Harlequin Romances

OTHER

Harlequin Romances

by MARJORIE LEWTY

To Catch a Butterfly

by

MARJORIE LEWTY

Harlequin Books

TORONTO • LONDON • NEW YORK • AMSTERDAM • SYDNEY • WINNIPEG

Original hardcover edition published in 1977
by Mills & Boon Limited

ISBN 0-373-02075-9

Harlequin edition published June 1977

CHAPTER ONE

IT was half past five on an afternoon in July and London was sweltering in a heat wave. In the typing room of the Ashbrook Secretarial Studio the temperature had been hovering around eighty since lunch, and the two girls who were still there, working on a long and boring directors' report, had knocked off briefly in an effort to cool down.

The younger one, whose name was Marilyn, slumped back in her swivel chair, fanning herself with a folded newspaper, and continued the conversation she had just started. 'You've simply got to be joking, Kate,' she said.

Kate Warrington, twenty-two, slim and lovely, with a straight little nose and cool grey eyes that looked out on the world as if they weren't often fooled by what they saw, grinned across the gap between their two desks. 'Not a bit of it,' she said. 'I'm dead serious.'

Marilyn shook her yellow curls in blank disbelief. 'You're saying that really—truly—you wouldn't marry a millionaire if you got the chance?'

'Really—truly.' Kate rolled a fresh piece of paper into her typewriter.

'Not even *him*?' Marilyn pushed the folded newspaper slyly under Kate's nose.

Kate glanced down at it and saw why Marilyn had brought up the subject of millionaires. At the top of the page was a photograph of a dark man with a straight mouth and long-lashed eyes whose magnetic quality not even poor newsprint could disguise. The face of a man who would get to the top no matter how many other men he shot down in the process, she thought with faint contempt. Below the photograph, the caption read:

'YOUNG MILLIONAIRE BRINGING HOME
THE DOLLARS?
Damian St Ewan, Cornish quarry owner, returns today
from Toronto with a provisional promise of the backing
he has been seeking from the Vestor Corporation of
Canada, which may run into seven figures. This should
mark another step along the way to the eventual re-
opening of the St Ewan tin mine, Wheal Dora, in West
Cornwall, where drilling operations have recently dis-
closed a considerable deposit of ore still remaining. Mr St
Ewan already owns one of the most successful slate
quarries in the country, and is involved in the financial
side of the new deal for the fishing industry at Polken-
nock.'

Kate handed back the paper without comment and turned
to her typewriter, but Marilyn wasn't to be put off. Her
plump face registered unabashed curiosity. 'That's the man
you went to take letters for last week, isn't it?'
'Yes, that's the man.' Kate's pretty mouth curled slightly.
So he had got what he was going to Canada for! She wasn't
in the least surprised. Damian St Ewan had struck her, even
in that one brief encounter, as a man who didn't expect to
fail in anything he undertook. 'One of our young financial
wizards,' Mrs Ashbrook had called him when she gave Kate
the assignment to go to his flat to deal with correspondence
he had been working on coming up in the train from Cornwall. 'One of the men who is going to put this country back
where it belongs—in the big league,' she added admiringly.
Mrs Ashbrook was dedicated to rich business men, which
wasn't surprising as they formed a large part of the dis-
tinguished clientele of the Ashbrook Secretarial Studio.
Kate's own opinion of tycoons was entirely different, for her
own good reasons which she didn't talk about.
'You never told me he was *that* fabulous,' sighed Marilyn.
'Wasn't it thrilling to work for him? Weren't you terribly
impressed?'
'Not terribly. It was just a job.' That wasn't strictly ac-

6

curate. She had been impressed, but not in the way Marilyn meant. As soon as she saw Damian St Ewan she had felt the dislike she always felt towards men like him, who lived to make money. The fact that he happened to be young and good-looking, and possessed a certain charm, only made matters worse, in her opinion. And the final, entirely unreasonable, thing she had against him was that he lived in Cornwall. Cornwall happened to be Kate's own magic land of dreams and it was all wrong that it should produce smooth tycoons like Damian St Ewan. But she wasn't going to explain her prejudices to Marilyn, who was just eighteen and obviously considered the typing studio a fount of romantic possibilities. Kate smiled at her and said, 'You've been watching too many old Hollywood movies.'

Marilyn sighed. 'P'raps you're right. Come to think of it, you're rather like the girl in the one I saw last night, Kate.' Her eyes went somewhat enviously to the neat figure under Kate's tricel dress. 'She seemed sort of cool too, just like you do, only actually'—she rolled her eyes expressively —'actually she wasn't a bit cool, if you follow me. Wow-ie!' She chuckled throatily. 'There was one scene in the jungle where she and this man——'

The sound of a telephone bell stopped her in mid-sentence. 'That was Mrs Ashbrook's phone, wasn't it? Mind if I dash off, Kate. I can finish this lot in ten minutes in the morning.' She was pushing sheets of paper into a drawer. 'I promised Norman I'd meet him at six and I daren't risk being out on a job this late. He gets mad if I keep him waiting.' She glanced apologetically at Kate. 'I'm not letting you down?'

'No, you run along. I'll hold the fort in case it's something urgent.'

One of the points that Mrs Ashbrook made clear when she engaged an applicant for a job was that they mustn't be clock-watchers. Visiting V.I.P.s from overseas, company directors, sales managers passing through London from the provinces, any of them might call up and demand the services of an expert typist for an hour or more at any odd

7

time of the day—or evening. *They* didn't spare themselves in the high-pressure game of big business. They were prepared to pay Mrs Ashbrook's top fees for girls who didn't spare themselves either. Kate considered the whole of the world of big business a howling desert, and as soon as she could afford it she had every intention of heading for a cottage in Cornwall, where her mother belonged, and leaving behind the rat-race and all who ran in it. But while she worked here, she worked conscientiously because that was the only way she knew.

Besides, before she could even consider getting away there was the Nanny problem to solve, and that was getting more pressing, not less. She opened her handbag now and unfolded the letter she had received from Nanny this morning.

'Dear Miss Kate,' Nanny had written. (Dear, funny, loyal, old-fashioned Nanny still called her 'Miss Kate' as she had done all these years, long after she had retired from service in Kate's family.) Thank you very much for your nice letter. We are quite well here, I am glad to say, except for Monty who went out on Saturday night and stayed out all night, the naughty boy, although I called and called. When he came home for his breakfast his ear was torn and bleeding and I had to take him to the vet. The vet said he should have been doctored when he was a kitten so he wouldn't go out at night, but I told him I was against it as I thought it was cruel, and the vet was quite nice and understanding and said that Monty was a fine cat and he must be good company for me when he didn't go out. He put something on Monty's ear and it is clearing up nicely now.

I had another letter from Mrs Gray's solicitor this morning and he says that they will soon have to get something settled about this house as it was left to Mrs Gray's nephew in her will and he wants to sell it as he needs the money. What do you think I should reply to them, Miss Kate? They can't turn me out, can they? I

8

don't understand these legal matters, but I have been thinking hard about it because I don't like to feel a trouble to anyone and Mrs Gray's nephew is a very nice young man and it is awkward to have to go against what he wants because after all the house belongs to him now. He came to see me last week and explained it all in quite a friendly way. Perhaps I could get into a nice Home somewhere. I shouldn't mind so very much for myself, only I don't think they would let me have Monty with me, would they?'

Here the shaky handwriting became more shaky. Kate folded the letter quickly and thrust it back into her handbag. Something must be done soon, but what? Nanny paid her rent promptly, but that wasn't going to be enough to guard against the prompting of her kind heart. The financial needs of Mrs Gray's very pleasant young nephew (about whom Kate had distinct doubts) would almost certainly get more pressing. Nanny would be persuaded to move out so that the house could be sold more easily without its sitting tenant, and where would she get a place to rent where she would be happy, and at a price she could afford? Nowhere, Kate's business experience told her. What was needed, she thought, rubbing her forehead where it was beginning to ache, was a kind fairy godmother.

Just then Mrs Ashbrook emerged from her office, and anything less like a fairy godmother could hardly have been imagined. She was fortyish, smartly dressed, elegantly haggard, and as hard as nails, the very pattern of a successful business woman, Kate always considered. But she treated her staff fairly, and Kate, who was always willing to work late if required to do so, was Mrs Ashbrook's favourite.

'Oh, Kate dear, you're still here, praise be!' At this time in the afternoon Mrs Ashbrook's make-up was inclined to cake and now it creased into a myriad tiny wrinkles as she smiled her relief. 'Mr St Ewan has just been on the phone, ringing from Heathrow. He's going straight back to his flat now, but he has to catch the night train to Cornwall and he's asking if you could spare him an hour or so before he leaves. I told him I'd see if you were available and he's going to ring back in a couple of minutes.'

'Me particularly?' Kate wasn't quite sure why she said that, for it was a normal thing for satisfied clients to ask for the same girl again.

'Yes, you particularly. He said if you weren't available he'd leave it.' Mrs Ashbrook sounded faintly puzzled, but Kate remembered that Mr St Ewan had a very positive way with him below his relaxed, deceptively lazy manner. He wasn't a man to be shy about insisting on getting something he wanted. Complete confidence, that was what you needed to get you to the top in the millionaire league. And complete ruthlessness, of course, she added mentally, with the sad empty feeling inside that she still got when she remembered what happened to her father, who hadn't been ruthless enough.

'Do you think you could possibly manage it, dear?' Mrs Ashbrook was looking more haggard than ever, but of course it would be very bad business to have to refuse a millionaire. 'I know you've done a lot of extra work lately, but I'd be awfully grateful if you could go.'

Kate pulled the paper out of her typewriter. 'Yes, I'll go. Certainly.' She stood up and smoothed the skirt of her pleated ivory dress. A little more overtime, a little more cash for the savings account—it all added up. But it wasn't going to be enough to solve Nanny's problem. 'The same place, I suppose?' She had a quick picture of a luxury service flat in a modern block near Green Park.

'Yes. Bless you, Kate, you're an angel.' Mrs Ashbrook's wrinkles smoothed out. 'Oh, there's the phone again now, the man's getting impatient.' She flew back towards her office, calling over her shoulder as she went, 'Take a taxi, I'll put it on his account.'

'You bet I will!' Kate's smile had a touch of malice in it, towards rich men in general and Damian St Ewan in particular.

10

Kate had been too optimistic about the taxi. The rush hour was well into its swing and every single taxi that came her way swooped past with its flag down. She was between tube stations, and anyway the idea of joining the mass of humanity crowding into the trains on a steaming hot afternoon appalled her. The queues for the buses were formidable. She hitched her white sling bag over her shoulder, tucked her briefcase under her arm, and set off along the length of Oxford Street.

The sun was still beating down as relentlessly as it had been all day. The pavements burned through the thin soles of her sandals, her fringe of dark hair clung damply to her forehead. There seemed to be no air, only the smell of petrol fumes and hot tar. Oh, for Cornwall! she thought, remembering with longing the deep blue sky and white spray on jagged rocks, the scream of gulls, the feel of clean wet wind on her cheeks. But it was futile really, the dreaming, because she wasn't going to have a holiday in Cornwall, not until she had paid back all she had borrowed from Nanny. Not that she could ever repay the debt she owed to Nanny, because there was far more than mere money involved.

There had been nothing at all left after the business failure that had put her father into the bankruptcy court three years ago, when Kate was eighteen, and surely brought about the heart attack that killed him. Her mother had been dead for many years and she had no other relatives. The friends in her own set had conveniently melted away when trouble struck. Most painful of all, Roger had backed out of their engagement. For a time Kate had quite literally wanted to die. It was Nanny who took her into her own small home and gave her love, and hope, and courage until she was able to stand on her own feet again. It was Nanny who used her own savings to pay for Kate's secretarial training at a top college in London.

'You're a clever girl, Miss Kate dear,' Nanny had insisted. 'You must have the very best training you can find, then you'll get a good job afterwards.'

Homely, practical advice, as homely and practical as

Nanny herself. It had proved good advice too. Kate had found the good job with Mrs Ashbrook. The pay was generous and she could have afforded a small flat for herself. Instead, she joined up with four other girls in a large, draughty old house in Highgate and settled down there to live as cheaply as possible and save hard until she could pay back the money that Nanny had spent on her. Only then would she be free to think about the life she really wanted, far away from the cut-throat world of finance and big business that had killed her father. But saving wasn't easy; there was the little matter of inflation, and living in London cost the earth. Likewise clothes, and you had to be reasonably well turned out so that you wouldn't let down the studio when you were sent out on assignment to some big house, or luxury flat, or one of the top hotels. No, she might as well face the fact that she wasn't going to be free for a long time, and there wasn't the slightest hope of getting to Cornwall. She would spend her summer holiday next month in Nanny's little house in Bristol, as she had done for the past three years. Always supposing, she thought with a pang, that Nanny still had her little house. The thought was so gloomy and so fraught with worry that she turned back again to pictures of tumbling seas and wild, empty moors and immediately felt a little better. At least it helped her along as she ploughed through the last of the rush-hour crowds in Regent Street and into Piccadilly, so that she reached the modern building where Mr St Ewan had his flat that much more painlessly.

Inside it was blessedly cooler, air-conditioned, of course. The caretaker consulted a board and told her that Mr St Ewan wasn't in, so Kate went into the ground-floor cloakroom to check on her make-up after that hot, dusty walk. She held her wrists under the cold tap, dabbed cheeks and forehead with cleansing tissues, patted her dark hair into its straight, no-nonsense style which she hoped made her appear calm and competent. Her silky dress, a shirtwaister in ivory tricel with a permanently pleated skirt and a wide suede belt, was unfussy and suited her neat figure and slender legs. Yes, she would do. Even on a grilling day she still had a look of the cool, unflappable secretary; she wouldn't let Mrs Ashbrook and the studio down. She gave herself a small, encouraging smile and went out to wait for the financial wizard himself, Mr Damian St Ewan.

He arrived ten minutes later. As he walked without haste across the entrance hall, dark and tall, and oozing the confidence and magnetism of the successful man from every inch of him, Kate felt the old familiar prickle of antagonism bristling down her spine as if she had been a defiant kitten. She recognised it for prejudice, but she couldn't help it. It was the same feeling that rich successful men always aroused in her—only more so. Probably because this man had more. He had everything, didn't he? Money, power, youth (he looked about thirty-two or three), stunning good looks, and the self-assurance of the devil. In fact he resembled pictures of the devil, when you came to look closer; it was probably the odd slope of his dark eyebrows. She watched him come nearer, noticing the custom-made peat-brown suit, the cream silk shirt with the dull gleam of gold links and wristwatch, the thick black hair brushed into an elegant, not over-long style. He looked as if he had emerged straight from the hands of his gentleman's gentleman, rather than having just jetted across the Atlantic. She disliked him intensely on principle, but her job demanded politeness, even deference.

She got to her feet as he reached her. 'Good afternoon, Mr St Ewan.'

He nodded easily. 'Miss Warrington. Good of you to come so promptly. Shall we go up?' He smiled a greeting at the caretaker, who saluted navy-fashion and opened the lift door for them.

It was one of the mini-lifts, designed to hold two. Kate squeezed into a corner as they were sucked silently up to the second floor. At close quarters this man's very presence seemed to pack such a potent, magnetic punch that she felt, absurdly, that she would be singed if she even brushed against him. The lift gate opened with an oiled swoosh on

13

to a square, carpeted landing. Damian St Ewan fitted his key into one of the four white doors opening off the landing and stood aside for her to enter the flat first. Polished manners, she thought, smooth and calculated like everything else about him.

She remembered the flat from last time. Not that there was anything particularly memorable about it. It was much the same as so many of these executive apartments she had visited during her time with Mrs Ashbrook—a luxury pied-à-terre in London for top men who kept their wives and families in the country and commuted for week-ends, when they weren't too busy putting through colossal takeovers. She wondered briefly what this man's wife was like. Beautiful and soignée and bored-looking, she guessed. She had met many of that sort of woman when her father was alive. In the two years between leaving school and the time that her world crashed about her, she had acted as his hostess, giving small dinner parties for his business acquaintances and their wives. Even then, although she had wanted to please him, she hadn't really enjoyed those parties or liked the people. Only Roger, of all her father's business friends, had been different, she believed. She had thought he had a scale of values that wasn't dependent on money. How wrong she had been!

Damian St Ewan put down his air-travel suitcase, indicated one of the deep, buttoned leather chairs and sat down opposite. For the first time she noticed that he looked faintly weary.

'I hope you had a successful trip, Mr St Ewan,' she murmured politely, unzipping her briefcase and taking her notebook out. Last time she came she had sat at the desk in the window, where the typewriter was, while he had dictated his letters, but she could probably manage just as well on her knee. She found her Biro and pretended to examine the working end of it, giving him time to marshal his thoughts. But when, after what seemed several minutes, he didn't produce any papers or say a word, she looked up expectantly, to see his eyes fixed on her in a curious, considering way as if he were thinking of anything rather than his business correspondence. Probably suffering from jet-lag, thought Kate. She knew it did funny things to your concentration.

At last he said, 'Put that notebook down, will you, it unnerves me. Let's have a drink first.' He eased himself out of his chair and strolled across the room to a built-in cupboard. 'What would you like? There seems to be everything here.'

Kate had a stock answer ready for invitations like this. 'A bitter lemon, please.'

He grimaced. 'Nothing more interesting?'

'No, thank you, that would be lovely,' she said firmly. It was one of the rules of the typewriting studio that you didn't accept drinks when you went out on a job, and even if it hadn't been, she would have made it her own rule. For one thing, you needed a clear head for secretarial work, and for another thing, as Mrs Ashbrook herself said, you could never be a hundred per cent sure about the men you were working for.

He brought their drinks and set them on a low table. From a gold cigar case he selected a slim cigar and lit it methodically. When it was going to his satisfaction he leaned back in his chair, crossed his long legs, and continued his observation of Kate from beneath lowered, heavily-fringed eyelids.

She began to feel vaguely uneasy. She sipped her drink, met his eyes momentarily and looked hastily down again. It would have taken a far more sophisticated girl than her to meet that brooding stare of his and hold it, and in any case they certainly weren't on terms like that. He was the big chief, she was the lowly secretary. Kate was no unfledged teenager, she had met all types of men and she had had her awkward moments, but she had never been scrutinised quite like this before. Just as if I were a slave girl up for auction, she told herself, working up her resentment against the man. She kept her eyes down, noticing in spite of herself the way the fine cloth of his trouser leg strained across his knee and fell into an immaculate crease down to the supple brown leather of handmade shoes. I bet I could keep myself in clothes for a year for what he spent on those shoes, she thought peevishly.

She had worked herself into such a fine state of petulance that when he finally spoke she got quite a shock. 'Miss Warrington,' he said. 'I know this is going to sound extremely personal, but I have my reasons. Would you object to telling me if you have any definite ties in London? Husband? Boy-friend? Any other—er—encumbrances?'

She was too startled to do anything but tell the truth 'No,' she replied, staring blankly.

'And are you still as keen to go to Cornwall as you were when you came here last?' It amazed her that he remembered. They had made small talk for a few minutes before she left, on the level of How-lovely-to-live-in-Cornwall-I'd-love-to-go-there-again. He couldn't have known about the real longing that lay beneath the conventional words. Or could he? Could perception on that scale be part of the secret of the success of men like this?

But whatever his game she wasn't going to join in. 'Of course,' she said lightly, impersonally. 'Who wouldn't, on an eighty in the shade day in London?'

'Quite,' he said, and he didn't smile back. 'Well then, I have a proposition to put to you.'

A sharp feeling like fear spiralled down inside her. So that *was* it! Certainly she hadn't judged him that type of man, but she heard the word 'proposition' and reacted with push-button speed. She was on her feet in a split second, grey eyes glinting dangerously. 'I came to take dictation, Mr St Ewan,' she said coldly. She reminded herself that even slave girls have their dignity and pulled herself a little straighter. 'May I go now, please?'

He raised dark eyebrows. 'Aren't you rather jumping the gun, Miss Warrington? But I apologise if my choice of words alarmed you. Let's say I have a *plan* that may interest you. Won't you sit down again and hear what it is?' He leaned forward and tapped the arm of her chair invitingly.

16

She felt her cheeks go warm. She wasn't sure whether he was actually trying to make her look a fool or whether he was achieving it without effort. Whichever it was, it increased her dislike of the man. Reluctantly she sat down on the edge of the chair.

'That's better.' Amusement lurked in his eyes, which only made her more angry than ever. 'Now, let's begin all over again, using words of one syllable that can't be misunderstood. *You* would like to go to Cornwall. *I* live there. *I* need help which *you* could give me. *So* it would seem a good plan to team up. There, how's that? Innocent enough for you?'

She stared at him, ignoring the irony. 'You mean—you're offering me a job in Cornwall?'

'Right. A temporary one, say a couple of months. You would have your ordinary salary from Mrs Ashbrook and, of course, all living and travelling expenses. Plus a bonus of—oh, four or five hundred. We could discuss that later.'

Two months in Cornwall, she thought, and closed her eyes. She felt quite faint with longing. But how could she go so far away for so long with this crisis about Nanny's house looming up?

He was watching her closely. 'What about it?'

'I don't know. It's been rather sudden.' Would two months really make any difference to Nanny's position? She could write and advise her not to do anything in a hurry, not to sign anything. She could tell her about rent tribunals and suggest that she should go to the Citizens' Advice people if she were really bothered. And there was this bonus he'd offered her. It sounded far too much, but of course what would a few hundred pounds mean to him? To her it would be a godsend if Nanny did have to move eventually. But she hadn't quite convinced herself yet. 'But surely you have your own secretary there, Mr St Ewan?'

'At my office in Truro, yes, I have. What I'm thinking of is someone to be available at my home over the next few weeks. Warren Lindsay, Vestor's top man, is visiting England himself shortly and there's going to be a press of extra work on this Wheal Dora project.' He seemed to linger on the

17

name almost lovingly. Wheal Dora might have been a glamorous girl, not a tin mine.

Kate still hesitated. 'But I don't quite understand. Why me? Surely you could find a secretary nearer your home?'

He looked her over slowly and deliberately, from her neat white sandals to her smooth dark head, lingering longest perhaps on her hands with their almond-shaped finger nails that Kate cared for so fastidiously, and the suede belt that clipped her dress in at the waist. At his look the colour threatened to rise into her cheeks again, but his tone was quite impersonal as he said, 'I'm sure you'll fill the bill admirably, Miss Warrington, and I haven't time to experiment. Can you be ready to come with me on the night train?'

She blinked. This was fast work, even for a high-powered tycoon. She shook her head doubtfully. 'I'd have to consult Mrs Ashbrook. And there would be my things to pack and arrangements to be made at my flat. I'm afraid——'

'I can't see any problem.' He stood up and went across to the phone. 'Do you have Mrs Ashbrook's number?'

She told him and watched him dial, perched on the desk, one long leg swinging casually. All trace of weariness had gone now. This was the goal-seeking, decision-making machine in action. It occurred to her that she hadn't actually agreed to take the job; he had bulldozed her into it. She looked at the straight mouth, the uncompromising jaw, and thought she could well understand why this man was on his way to his second—or third, or fourth—million.

She listened to him turning his masterful charm on Mrs Ashbrook and in no time at all it was clear that she was practically eating out of his hand.

He passed the receiver over to Kate. 'Have a word yourself.'

Mrs Ashbrook's gratification at this turn of events came across the wire unmistakably. 'Of course I can spare you, my dear. I'm always glad for you girls to take temporary work outside the studio, it broadens your outlook and it's good for the reputation of the studio as well. And

it's quite an honour for you to be chosen by Mr St Ewan.
I can assure you. Quite frankly, Kate, I might have reserva-
tions about sending you off like this with some of the men
clients, but not Mr St Ewan. I'm certain he is a perfect
gentleman.'

'Are you?' said Kate, looking towards the subject of their
conversation, who had seated himself in his chair again and
was following all this closely.

'Yes, Kate, I am,' Mrs Ashbrook insisted. 'I know it's
supposed to be out of date, but I mean in the true sense of
the word. He belongs to a very old Cornish family—I always
check on my clients. Well, I won't expect you back until I
hear from you—and mind you do the studio credit.' She
laughed archly. 'I'm sure I can trust you to do that.'

'I hope so, Mrs Ashbrook. Goodbye for the present, then.'
She replaced the receiver slowly and looked down at it,
feeling as if her last link with reality had been broken.

She looked across to the man in the chair and he cocked
an eyebrow. 'Well? Did the worthy lady give me a good
character?'

'She assured me that you were a perfect gentleman.'

His mouth twitched. 'And being a good little employee,
you're willing to take her word for it?'

This odious way of his of making her look foolish was
something she would have to get used to, she supposed.
Get used to, but not necessarily submit to. Her grey eyes
were very cool as she replied, with a note of disdain that she
was hardly aware of herself, 'I've agreed to work for you
temporarily, Mr St Ewan. I can only hope that Mrs Ashbrook
is justified in her opinion.'

His dark eyebrows lifted and at the same time drew together in the middle, giving him a distinctly devilish look.
'I hope so too,' he said.

Suddenly he became very businesslike. 'Now we'll do
some organising.' He came back to the telephone and she
retired quickly to the middle of the room. 'Paddington first,'
he said. 'Here's hoping they can book us an extra sleeper.
We may be lucky as it's mid-week. I'd offer you mine, only

that wouldn't do. I rather think British Rail still have old-fashioned views about segregating the sexes on these occasions.'

Kate said confusedly, 'It doesn't really matter about a sleeper for me. I can sleep anywhere—I'm not fussy.' Too late she realised the absurd implication of the words and hoped he wouldn't notice.

But of course he did. He stood with the receiver to his ear, waiting for a reply, surveying her narrowly. 'No? You surprise me,' he drawled. 'That wasn't the impression you gave me recently. If there's no berth available for you we'll have to put up here for the night and catch the early train in the morning.'

'You could travel tonight and I could follow on tomorrow,' she said quickly. Even now she had a hazy idea of thinking it over, perhaps backing out.

He shook his head, reading her mind accurately. 'Oh no, you don't, Miss Warrington. You're committed now. I shall keep an eye on you until we're safely on the train.' The station booking office answered the call then and she was left with a feeling of complete helplessness. This maddening individual seemed to hold all the best cards and never missed a trick.

He got the reservation, of course. She would have been amazed if he hadn't. It seemed that the name of St Ewan was a kind of 'Open Sesame' to all doors.

He replaced the receiver. 'Good! They found they had a cancellation.'

'Naturally,' said Kate dryly.

He shot her a quick frowning glance but didn't respond to that. She would have to watch it, Kate thought. This was not a man you could needle and get away with it.

'Your turn now, Miss Warrington.' He indicated the phone. 'While I'm tidying up you might get on to the Great Western Hotel and book a table for us in the restaurant. We may as well dine there and then we can get straight on to the train. They usually do a very good steak, too. Oh, and buzz down to Parker, will you—that's the intercomm on the wall there. Tell him I'm leaving a pile of laundry on the bed for the kind attention of his good wife.' He smiled briefly. 'Use a bit of the old charm with Parker, he loves it. He's a nice old bird, ex-naval and proud of it, and he and his wife are invaluable to me. Ask him if he'll rustle up a cab for us, in about five minutes. We'll go to your flat so that you can pack, and then straight on to Paddington.' He picked up his travelling case and left her.

In a kind of daze Kate did as he had told her. She was beginning to wonder if she would be able to keep up the breakneck pace which she had no doubt he would set. She had just had a glimpse of the dynamic drive which she had suspected lay under the relaxed, unhurried manner of her new employer and guessed that he wouldn't be an easy man to satisfy. Her opinion of him had not changed a bit. Quite the reverse, in fact. The more she saw of him the more she resented him, as she resented any man who manipulated others quite ruthlessly for their own egotistic purposes. She had no doubt at all that that was exactly what he had done with her.

Just so long as she recognised all this, and wasn't likely to be taken in by him, all would be well, she believed. For the sake of two months in Cornwall she was prepared to put up with a good deal.

How much she had no way of knowing.

CHAPTER TWO

THE taxi deposited them before a tall old house in Highgate. Damian St Ewan told the driver to wait and, tucking his slim travelling satchel under his arm, followed Kate up to the second floor.

'I must warn you, five of us live here,' she told him as she put her key into the lock.

'Five? Don't you find that a bit of a crush?'

21

'We like it,' she said coolly. He might be going to employ her, but that didn't give him the right to patronise her. All the same, she rather hoped that none of the other girls was in yet.

She pushed open the door. 'Do come in.' She was somewhat out of practice at being a gracious hostess. She glanced into the large, sprawling sitting room and winced as she saw the piles of theatre magazines littering the floor, the remains of someone's lunch on the table, the loose cover ballooning out from the lumpy settee. But there was nothing to be done except put the best face she could on it all. She led the way into the sitting room. 'Won't you sit down? I'll try not to be long. Perhaps you'd care for a drink while you're waiting?' What did you offer a millionaire to drink? Coke? Plonk? She very nearly burst into a giggle at the idea.

He sat down in the fireside chair with the bulging spring. 'Thanks, I think I'll save up for dinner. We'll get along to the hotel as soon as you're ready.'

'Just as you like,' said Kate, relieved. 'I'll go and pack, then.'

In the bedroom she shared with Maxie, she took her one and only suitcase down from the top of the wardrobe, dusted it off and opened it on the bed. Packing wouldn't take long. She was reasonably tidy by nature—or, more likely, because of Nanny's early training—and everything she possessed was newly washed and neatly stacked in drawers, or hung on her side of the wardrobe. Maxie's side was chaotic, but Maxie was an aspiring actress and not particularly systematic. She always managed to look marvellous when she was ready to go out, and that was the important thing. Into Kate's suitcase went undies and tights, nighties and slippers, a frothy blue wrap. Trousers, a couple of woollies, the three summer dresses that she possessed as well as the one she was wearing. She was hardly likely to need a long dress for evenings—she was going to work, not on a social visit—but she put her one and only long dress in, just in case. It was three years old, a leftover from the old days when she had far more clothes than

22

she needed. (But Father encouraged her to spend money on them. 'I like to show off my pretty daughter,' he would say.) She spread it out on the bed to fold and sighed as she touched the supple Liberty silk patterned in yellow, burnt orange and pale mint green. It had cost as much as she would spend on five dresses now. But it was no good sighing, she told herself, because expensive clothes didn't fit in with the new life she had mapped out for herself in the future. Model dresses don't go with a country cottage and growing your own vegetables!

She was taking a light tweed coat off its hanger when the door opened and Maxie draped herself across the entrance, striking a theatrical pose as she always did. Kate was never quite sure how much of Maxie was pose and how much wasn't; sometimes she thought that Maxie didn't know herself. But however that might be, she was beautiful —a natural silver blonde with a figure that drew response from any male in sight, ranging from wolf whistles to dinner dates. She floated across the bedroom now, gorgeous in a wispy black confection and scarlet sandals, and stared significantly at Kate's open suitcase.

'Ah-ha!' she breathed conspiratorially. 'And what is our quiet little Kate up to now? And who, if you please, is that fantastic male animal I caught a glimpse of in the sitting room as I came through? Can it be true that you've fallen at last, darling?' Kate had a reputation with her flatmates for being very choosy who she went out with. She wasn't very keen on parties either. But they were an easy-going bunch of girls and took each other pretty much for granted. Kate was the quiet one, the introvert, and that was that. She had never told any of them what had happened to make her that way, nor of the dream she held somewhere in the region of her heart; the dream of a cottage in Cornwall with a pram under the apple tree and a big, husky, sunbronzed countryman digging the vegetable patch. They would have giggled at that.

'Not what you're thinking, Maxie,' she said now. 'I'm going off to Cornwall on a job of work. Quite innocent.'

Maxie tilted her head and her silver hair fell on to one shoulder. 'With *him*? Now that's very interesting. *Very* interesting indeed!'

'You,' Kate told her calmly, 'have a nasty, suspicious mind, my sweet.' She tucked a pair of pumps down the side of her case. 'By the way, this job may last a few weeks. Tell Joan I'll send her a cheque for the rent, will you? And I'm sorry about having to leave my share of the chores.'

Maxie waved a white hand airily. 'Think nothing of it, darling. Now, aren't you going to introduce me to the boy-friend?'

Kate hesitated. 'Look, Maxie, he's not one of us, you know. He's in the top league.'

Maxie's smile flashed wickedly. 'He's a man, isn't he?'

There was no getting out of it. Kate shrugged, checked her suitcase, threw a light summer coat over her arm and led the way back to the sitting room.

Damian St Ewan got to his feet as soon as they came in. He seemed to dominate the big room with his height and his air of complete self-assurance. His eyes went over Kate's shoulder to Maxie, and Kate waited for the usual masculine reaction, but there was nothing. He just looked at Maxie and that was all; she might have been a chair or a table.

Kate murmured an introduction and Maxie moved close to him with just the merest sway of her lovely hips. 'Hullo, Mr St Ewan,' she breathed, and touched her lips with the tip of her tongue. Oh lord, she's overdoing it, thought Kate, embarrassed. In encounters with women Damian St Ewan would make his own rules, and *he* would call the tune, she felt sure of that.

He nodded with absent courtesy. 'How do you do, Miss Gladwin.'

Maxie wasn't particularly quick on the uptake; perhaps with her looks she didn't have to be. But sometimes Kate got the idea that even after three years at drama school she was more vulnerable than she appeared.

She fluttered the black satin crescents of her eyelashes

up at him. 'Are we all going to have coffee before you go, h'm?'

'Sorry,' he said, still polite. 'We must be on our way.'

Still Maxie couldn't believe that she was being snubbed. She put the tips of her fingers on his arm with a pretty pout. 'I won't let you go yet, not when you've only just come.'

His face hardened. Before this, Kate had only guessed at the steeliness that must surely be there underneath that almost lazy manner. But now he was letting it show. He looked at Maxie briefly, dismissively, then he turned to Kate. 'Shall we go, Miss Warrington?' He picked up her suitcase and walked over to open the door for her.

Heavens, but he was arrogant, thought Kate. She wouldn't have cared to invite a brush-off like that herself. Perhaps Maxie *had* invited it, but Kate couldn't help feeling sorry for her. With a little shrug towards the other girl that said, 'I warned you, didn't I?' she passed ahead down the stairs and into the waiting taxi.

As they swung into Kentish Town Road and headed for Paddington there was a small and—to Kate—uncomfortable silence. She was still prickling on Maxie's behalf. Couldn't he see she was just a rather silly kid? Did he have to be so crushing? Finally she felt she just had to say something in Maxie's defence.

'Maxine has only recently finished at drama school,' she told him. 'She's looking for her first part.'

'Oh yes?' He gave her a blank look and she saw that he had forgotten about poor Maxie already. She might have been an insect he had brushed off his sleeve. He rested his head against the back of the seat and said, 'God, I'm hungry. I can never eat on a plane. I shan't be even part-way human until I've fed.'

Human! He wouldn't know what the word meant. She was glad he was hungry, it served him right. If he was stupid enough to spend his time jetting round the world in the pursuit of more money than he knew what to do with, then that was his lookout. She threw him a glance full of contempt, but it missed its mark, for his eyes were closed.

In spite of herself she went on looking at him, curious about this man she was going to work with in that objective and yet strangely intimate relationship of personal secretary. In repose his face didn't soften at all. She saw the powerful dominance in it, the deep grooves between his brows, the straight line of his mouth, the uncompromising angle of his jaw, now with a faint dark shadow on it. What sort of a man was there behind the mask of the financial wizard, the clever manipulator of people? Was he in love with his wife? Did she love him?

Then with a shock she saw that his eyes were open, dark glittering slits under lowered lids. 'Well,' he asked her laconically, 'what's the verdict?'

'I—don't know what you mean.'

'I think you do, Miss Warrington. You were trying to decide what sort of man I am, weren't you?'

'Well, is that so strange?' She struggled for composure under the inspection of those dark probing eyes. 'The first thing a secretary needs to do is to get to know the man she's working for.'

'Highly commendable,' he drawled. 'I can see you're going to be even more efficient than I'd supposed. Shall I give you a few pointers to start you off? Let's see. I have a happy, even disposition. I'm responsible, broadminded, kind, affectionate, fond of children and animals. How's that to be going on with?'

'H'm,' she said.

'Too good to be true? Very well, let's modify it a little. I do not suffer fools gladly, as you may have noticed. I'm normally sweet-tempered, but I can be rather nasty when provoked. Oh, and incidentally, I'm not married.'

She gasped. 'I wasn't——'

'Oh, yes, you were,' he said urbanely. 'That's still the question that all women want to ask even in these days of so-called sex equality.' He closed his eyes again, denoting that the conversation was at an end.

Kate clenched her hands and stared out of the taxi window, seeing nothing. If he weren't her employer—if they

26

could meet on equal terms——! Her imagination spun round wildly, full of biting phrases, withering replies. Forlorn hope, she was no match for him and never would be, and in any case she was the secretary and he was the big boss, and that was of the essence. Ah well, she could at least dream of reducing him to size.

The taxi set them down at Paddington Station and Damian St Ewan said, 'We'd better pick up your ticket and reservation first.'

Kate stood a little way apart, waiting until he had transacted his business at the first class booking office. He joined her after a minute or two, looking satisfied. 'All fixed up. We were lucky to get that berth, it seems.'

She glanced at him as he stood tucking five-pound notes away in his wallet. The power of money! If you could afford to travel first-class through life you could get anything you wanted.

'Now,' he said, 'comes the big moment. We eat.' And he set off at a cracking pace towards the entrance to the Great Western Hotel.

Kate knew the Great Western quite well. Her journey to boarding school had started at Paddington and very occasionally, when he could spare time from his business engagements, her father had given her dinner here and seen her off on the train. Those were red-letter occasions. Usually Nanny came with her, and later on, after Nanny had retired, she managed things on her own.

It was strange to be walking up the long flight of stairs from the platform level with this stranger beside her. 'You always travel by train?' she asked him as they made their way to the restaurant.

He nodded. 'Nearly always. Usually by sleeper, it saves time.'

'And time is money, isn't it?' The words came out before she could stop them, with a bitter little edge. Her father's words, and his usual excuse for leaving her to grow up on her own. She thought fleetingly what fun they could have had together if he hadn't always been so overworked, so worried. What a lot he missed!

Damian St Ewan glanced down at her, his eyes nearly veiled by their long black lashes. 'Exactly,' he said blandly as they passed into the restaurant.

Kate had found it much too hot to eat at lunch time. Now, as they were escorted between the tables of diners, with the mouth-watering smell of good food in the air, the clink of wine glasses, the discreet hum of conversation, she realised how hungry she was. It was a long, long time since she had eaten out at any place more expensive than a Wimpey Bar.

Except for the ordinary politenesses of ordering a meal they began in silence, and that suited Kate very well. She noticed the covertly interested looks that her partner was attracting from the women among the diners around them, and thought with amusement that if this had been a romantic dinner date instead of a business arrangement she would have been pleased and flattered to be dining with such an eye-catching male. As it was, she was far more interested in the avocado that had just been placed before her, nestling in its bed of crushed ice.

She had left the ordering to her host, and predictably he had chosen fillet steak, with all the trimmings. In the recent past fillet steak had been, to Kate, merely a remembered delight, something occasionally noticed on the back counter at the butcher's, when she went in to buy mince for Spaghetti Bolognaise. Now, as the plate was put before her with its plump succulent contents, accompanied by a dark, rich and mysterious sauce, and she was helped liberally to sauté potatoes and petits pois, she sniffed with delicate appreciation. 'Super!' she breathed. 'I feel just like a starving Bisto kid.'

That was a pretty feeble remark, wasn't it? What on earth was she thinking of? You didn't really say things like that to your employer when you were being taken out on a business dinner, did you? She glanced across the table apprehensively and saw a faintly ironic grin on his face.

'Well done!' he remarked. 'I was beginning to wonder if you were capable of smiling, Miss Warrington. It's wonderful what a good steak can do.'

'Yes, isn't it?' she agreed crisply. Just for a moment she had imagined that he was going to share the joke, to show some proof that he was human, after all. But he had merely made it an excuse to score over her again and make her feel small. She might have known. All right then, if that was the way he liked to treat his employees, then she would know what to expect. She wouldn't say another word. Neither would she let this atrocious man spoil her dinner.

She didn't, either. The fillet steak was as tender and delicious as it looked and smelled, and the fresh raspberries and cream that followed sheer velvet delight. Beyond inquiring whether she would like more wine the man opposite applied himself to his food with enthusiasm and didn't attempt to make conversation, and that suited Kate very well. This shared meal was inevitable, she supposed, but once they reached their destination she wouldn't have to meet him socially, she hoped, and that would make it easier all round. Obviously he considered her a bore as a dinner partner, just as she considered him insufferably rude.

'Coffee in the lounge?' he suggested, finishing the last biscuit with a hunk of cheese. 'It'll be an hour or so before we can get into the train, so we may as well make ourselves comfortable.'

She didn't want to make herself comfortable with him. in the lounge or anywhere else, though she yearned for coffee. 'I think, if you'll excuse me, I'll have to skip coffee. I have a rather urgent letter I'd like to get written, if that's all right with you—sir.'

He shrugged. 'As you wish. I'll show you the way to the writing room.' He got up and pulled back her chair and as she rose to her feet her shoulder somehow brushed against his arm. Through the fine cloth of his jacket she could feel the hard muscle and bone and she drew away as if the contact had actually hurt. 'Don't trouble, I know my way,' she said hastily.

29

He looked rather hard at her, then he shrugged. 'You'll find me in the bar when you've finished, then—I take it you can find your way there, too?'

'I expect I can ask someone,' she said sweetly.

His eyes narrowed, she caught the glint of anger in them. Then he said quite gently, 'You do that. Oh, and by the way'—as she turned—'for Pete's sake don't call me sir. It's not that sort of job.'

Kate fled out of the restaurant and towards the writing room. As her feet stumbled over the vast expanse of soft carpet she found herself repeating, 'It's not that sort of job. It's not that sort of job.' What sort of job was it, then?

The writing room was empty. She sank into a chair at one of the tables, pulled paper towards her and began 'Dear Nanny——' She would write a long letter of reassurance to Nanny. She would explain about having to go to Cornwall, say she would phone as soon as she got there, warn her not to agree to anything about selling the house, and particularly not to sign any document of any sort until she, Kate, got back. She would set her mind at rest about the legal position and try to impress on her that there was nothing to worry about at the moment. She had paid her rent regularly and nobody could force her to leave. Yes, she would settle down to write a lengthy, loving letter and take as long as she could over it, before she had to go and seek out the St Ewan man.

She didn't have to seek him out; he came into the writing room just as she was sealing the envelope. He strolled across and rested both hands on the writing table, looking down at her. 'Finished?'

'Yes,' she said, getting her wallet out of her handbag for a stamp. She wished he wouldn't stand so close, it made her nervous. So nervous, in fact, that her hands shook and she fumbled with the tiny catch of the wallet. She pushed and pulled and wriggled it, but it was well and truly jammed.

'Let me try,' he offered, and took it from her. The catch sprang open at his touch and he handed it back.

'It does stick sometimes,' she said, wildly searching the pockets for a stamp, and remembering too late that she had used the last one yesterday when she sent off the gas bill.

He was still waiting patiently. Her head was on a level with the middle button of his brown jacket, so close that she could see the thread it was stitched on with, she could discern a faint tang of some masculine toilet preparation, probably from the handkerchief that protruded from his pocket. For a treacherous moment she was conscious of a stirring of attraction, a purely physical response to a man whom in every other way she disliked intensely. She felt weak with surprise and confusion.

'No stamp?' He took out his own wallet, extracted a stamp and held it out to her. 'Have one of mine.'

'Oh—thank you.' She reached to take it from him and inevitably their hands touched. To Kate, at that moment, it felt like touching a live electric wire and she promptly dropped the stamp on the floor. She leaned down to pick it up at the same moment that he did, and ridiculously their heads almost collided.

'Steady on,' he said, both his hands on her shoulders. He straightened her up in her chair and still held her, looking down in amusement at her flushed cheeks. 'You *are* an impetuous young woman, aren't you, Miss Warrington?' he said. 'You'd better let me attend to it for you.' He took the sealed envelope from the writing table, stuck the stamp on it, and slipped it in his pocket. 'We'll post this on our way,' he said. 'If you're ready we can get on to our train now and turn in. I don't know about you, but I'd be glad of a good long sleep.'

They went out of the writing room together. Kate wasn't sure, but she had a distinct feeling that he had looked at the address on the envelope as he stamped the letter. Why on earth should he want to know who she was writing to? She was sure he would stop at nothing to further his own interests where business was concerned, but her private life could hardly matter to him. Oh well, perhaps she had been mistaken; she was just naturally suspicious about him

31

and everything he did or said, but she mustn't let herself get neurotic about it. Also she must put a strong guard on her physical reactions where he was concerned or the next two months would prove unbearable. She dismissed the matter from her mind as they went out to the train.

At this time of night there were few people about. Kate always found stations rather frightening at night, somehow, empty and echoing. She shivered as they walked down the long platform, gripped again by the strangeness of this thing she was embarking on.

'Cold?' The man at her side looked down at her. 'You're very pale,' he said. 'You're all right, are you?' She thought he sounded almost concerned, but of course it would be a nuisance for him if she chose this moment to feel unwell.

'I'm fine,' she said. 'It's only the effect of the lighting.'

Damian St Ewan found the sleeping car attendant and handed over Kate's suitcase. He wasn't taking any chances, she thought, half amused. He had said he intended to keep an eye on her until they were in the train and he was doing just that. When there was something he wanted he left nothing to chance.

They stood together on the long, almost empty platform. 'I'd suggest turning in straight away,' he said. 'I hope you'll be comfortable.'

'I'm sure I shall be,' she said. Whatever people said about British Rail nobody could complain about the first-class sleeping accommodation, as she well remembered. But of course this man wasn't to know that only three years ago first-class travel was as much a part of her life as it was of his, and she had no intention of telling him. To him she was just a small-time secretary from a typing bureau and that was how she wanted it to remain.

He nodded. 'We meet at eight, then.' He looked down at her with a half smile that she found it impossible to inter-pret and again she was conscious of the disturbing effect his presence was having on her. Perhaps, she thought wryly, little Marilyn from the typing studio had something when she talked about jungle romance.

She pulled herself together and met his formal smile with one of her own, just as formal. 'I'll be ready,' she said.

He nodded once more, in approval this time. 'Good. Thank you for being so accommodating about everything, Miss Warrington. Sleep well.'

He strode away down the long platform to find his own compartment. She stood for a moment, watching his tall figure and broad back. He had probably had very little sleep for forty-eight hours or more—he had said he never slept on a plane—and yet his step was elastic, almost athletic. There was a tremendous reserve of strength and power about the man. No doubt he had learned how to protect that reserve, to relax when nothing of importance was happening, to react with split second timing and absolute control when required. Men who had reached the very top had learned to handle themselves, that was the secret of success. Everything calculated. Everything worked out to suit their own needs and convenience, to get what they willed to get. She smiled to herself. He would be mildly surprised if he knew how easily she could read him; how much she had learned through bitter experience about his type of man.

She shrugged and climbed into the train. The one thing that mattered was that in eight hours or a little more she would be back in her beloved Cornwall. Beside that blissful prospect nothing else was really important, certainly not Damian St Ewan.

In the tiny, self-contained compartment she took her time over undressing and washing. After the heat and excitement of the day it was heavenly to slip out of her clothes and between the cool, smooth sheets. As departure time approached the noises outside increased; steps in the corridor passed her curtained windows as other passengers claimed their berths. There was the sound of voices, laughter. The whole train quivered as diesel engines were turned on. An odd sense of excitement began to pervade everything, like the thrill that marks the curtain going up on a play.

Kate stretched out luxuriously and yawned and reminded

33

herself that what lay ahead was no play but a job of work, and no doubt a very demanding job at that, if she knew anything about Mr Damian St Ewan.

It was no good trying to go to sleep with all the clatter going on outside. She would lie still and think about Cornwall. She had only to close her eyes and it would all be there as it always was—the sea and the rocks and the yellow sand; the moors and the gulls; the high-banked narrow lanes; the little harbours and the sandy sheltered coves; the grey cottages straggling up steep village streets. Everything.

She closed her eyes and it was all there, just as usual. Then the picture became vague, changed, went out of focus. If she hadn't been so sleepy she would have been angry to realise that as she drifted into oblivion the colour film that was being projected inside her mind was of a big, broad-shouldered man with hair as black as a raven's wing, with mocking eyes and a mouth that could harden into contempt or twitch with amusement at some private joke of his own. A man who would sweep anything—or anyone—out of his way to get what he wanted. The kind of man she feared and hated.

Kate should have had nightmares that night. But, strangely enough, she slept without being conscious of dreaming at all, and the rhythmical pulse of train wheels on metals, as they bore her nearer and nearer to Cornwall, was like a lullaby.

CHAPTER THREE

THE train was punctual and so was Kate. At eight o'clock next morning she was out on the platform at Penzance, wearing slacks and a warm sweater and taking her first rapturous sniff of Cornish air for thirteen years. Not that the air was all that different from the air in any other railway station; she just imagined it was.

Almost at once she saw the tall figure of Damian St Ewan at the far end of the platform. It was a long train and he took quite a time to reach her, dodging piles of luggage and knots of disembarking passengers, his dark head and brown face towering above everyone else. Quite suddenly, as she stood waiting for him, she felt a strong tug of excitement inside her, almost as if he had been her lover striding towards her, big and handsome and thrilling. How ridiculous could you get? She must be a little drunk on Cornish air already, she thought dizzily.

He had reached her now. 'Good morning, Miss Warrington. Sleep well?' He didn't stop or wait for a reply. He picked up her suitcase and strode on towards the station exit, saying over his shoulder, 'We're being met, I hope. That is, if my major-domo didn't oversleep.'

'Your what?' asked Kate, scuttling after him towards the car park. She might as well follow up any clues that would give her a line on the household she was about to enter.

'Major-domo. The man who does everything I don't have the time to do myself. Ah, there he is,' as a stocky, red-haired young man with a swathe of freckles across his pleasant face approached them.

'You made it, then, Hugo,' Damian St Ewan said. 'Nice work.'

The young man grinned cheerfully. 'Only just. The alarm clock let me down again. Good trip?'

'Tolerable,' said Damian St Ewan. 'It's good to be home again, though.' He seemed to remember Kate, who was standing meekly behind him. 'This is Hugo Harris, my second-in-command, Miss Warrington,' he said.

She took the large hand that was held out to her and replied with a smile to the red-haired man's greeting and the three of them walked across to the car park on the harbour wall. From here Kate got her first glimpse of the sea and she stopped still while the two men went on ahead, savouring her moment of delight when a dream began to come true.

35

It amazed her that she had remembered it all so well—the colour of the water, the boats riding at anchor, the grey stone of the old sea wall, the white puffy clouds riding in a blue sky, the caress of the cool morning air on her face. It was almost too wonderful to be true. But she was here to work, she reminded herself, and hurried after the others.

There were only a few cars parked and she immediately picked out the one that must be a millionaire's car—a superb, silver-grey, low-slung Rolls-Royce coupé. Hugo was leading the way and as they reached the Rolls she expected him to stop, but to her surprise he walked on and opened the door of a Range Rover that was standing a little further away.

'You'd like to drive, Mr St Ewan?' Hugo seemed to know the answer already, for he was loading Kate's suitcase into the back and getting in after it.

Damian St Ewan swung himself up behind the wheel, leaned over and held out a hand to Kate. 'Want a lift up? It's quite a step.'

She took his hand because she couldn't very well refuse, and again she was conscious of that little throb of her pulse at his touch. His hand felt hard and strong as he pulled her up into the seat beside him, and the skin was unexpectedly harsh. Strange that, when everything else about him was so smooth and immaculate. Maybe he took his exercise heaving slates in his own quarry, she thought, suppressing a giggle as she glanced at the knife-crease in his brown trousers, the gold cuff links in the cream silk shirt, the fine supple leather of the shoes that were settling themselves on the controls of the big powerful vehicle.

Just then a commanding-looking man with curly grey hair, carrying a bulging briefcase stopped beside the silver-grey Rolls, fumbling in his pocket for his car keys. He saw Damian St Ewan and lifted a hand in greeting.

'Hullo, Damian. Didn't see you on the train.'

'Morning, John, how's everything?'

'Fine. Fine.' The voice matched the man, large, hearty and booming. 'I see you got things moving in Toronto.

Nice work! You back home for a spell?' It seemed to Kate that he shot an inquiring glance in her direction, but Damian St Ewan did not appear to notice.

'As long as I can manage,' he said.

'Good.' The grey-haired man opened the door of the Rolls. 'I'm off to New Zealand myself in a couple of weeks. No rest for the wicked!' He laughed heartily. 'I may take Carole with me for the ride. I'll tell her you're back, she'll be tickled to bits,' he added with a schoolboy grin. 'We must arrange a get-together before we leave.' Again he glanced at Kate. Then he lifted a large hand in salute before getting into the Rolls and manoeuvring it out of the car park.

Damian St Ewan sat in silent thought for a few moments before he let in the clutch of the Range Rover and eased the big, purring vehicle out towards the street. 'A neighbour of ours,' he threw the information casually at Kate. 'Big man in the china clay industry. Eh, Hugo?'

'And how!' came the succinct comment from the back.

And who was Carole? Kate found herself wondering. It couldn't be his wife. It would have to be his daughter who was tickled to death at Damian St Ewan's return. Anybody's daughter would be, of course, this man would attract girls by the dozen everywhere he went. She looked at his brown, competent hands on the wheel of the big powerful vehicle and found herself wondering what sort of lover he would make. Demanding and masterful and exciting, she thought, and then as she realised the route her thoughts were taking she began to feel warm all over. Disgraceful, she scolded herself with a suppressed grin. Nice girls aren't supposed to think about men in the way men think about girls.

'We'll go by the coast, round through Marazion,' he said, and the sudden sound of his deep voice breaking the silence made her catch her breath in acute embarrassment, just as if he could have known what she was thinking about. 'Miss Warrington's longing for a sight of the sea, aren't you?'

'Oh yes, I am,' she agreed fervently, and because she was suddenly unbearably conscious of the nearness of the man beside her she half turned towards Hugo, in the back. 'I spent an absolutely unforgettable holiday in Cornwall when I was a child.' She rushed quickly into explanations. 'I've been wanting to see it again ever since, but somehow I've never managed to get here. My mother was Cornish too, that's another reason.'

Hugo was obviously pleased to chat on about Cornwall. He was knowledgeable too. As they drove along the sea front approaching Marazion, with the wide blue sweep of Mount's Bay behind the sandhills on their right, and St Michael's Mount rising out of the sea, with its superb castle on the top, he told her a little of the story of the place; how it had been private residence, military fort, Benedictine chapel, in turn, going right back into the ancient past when the mount had been used by Celtic invaders who settled in Cornwall, to load ships with tin for the Mediterranean. 'But Mr St Ewan can tell you more about it than I can,' Hugo said. 'He's the expert on Cornish history.'

Kate murmured something non-committal; it surprised her to hear that the man beside her had time to be interested in anything more than his own business concerns. The man himself made no comment. He was driving carefully through the little town of Marazion itself now. Although there were few people about, this early in the morning, the twists and turns in the narrow streets had, no doubt, to be treated with respect by the Range Rover. Once through the town he turned off to the left and increased speed. Kate wondered where they were making for; she had no idea, of course, where his house was situated and it seemed a little odd to ask him, with Hugo sitting in the back. That was another awkward thing. When he introduced her to Hugo no mention had been made of the fact that she was a new secretary, and from the way Hugo behaved she somehow got the impression that he took it for granted that she was a girl-friend of his employer's, brought back from London for a visit. It put her in rather a false position, but no doubt it could be straightened out later. Meanwhile she settled down to enjoy the drive along the quiet country roads and through the tiny villages with their grey stone and slate cottages. As time passed they seemed to be getting deeper and deeper into the centre of Cornwall, the real Cornwall that was untouched by holidaymakers and the tourist trade. Kate sat silent, fascinated, drinking it all in, loving every minute of it. Her mother's home, where they had spent that unforgettable summer when Kate was eleven, was buried away deep in the countryside, and although it probably wasn't anywhere near here—in fact Kate had no clear idea where it was—she had a strong sense of homecoming.

The silence was broken when the man at the wheel glanced sideways at her and said, with what she took to be a touch of irony, 'Well, is it all as wonderful as you thought it would be?'

They were out on an open road now, a rather bare little road that climbed upwards, not particularly beautiful, with scrubby fields in one direction and a stone wall on the other. 'Yes,' breathed Kate ecstatically. 'Oh yes, it's better. It's all marvellous.' She saw his mouth twitch. He must think she was putting on an act; he would despise that, just as he had despised poor Maxie. Well, she couldn't help what he thought. 'I mean that,' she added firmly. 'I mean every word of it.'

The dark eyebrows went up a fraction. 'Of course you do, why shouldn't you? That's the way I always feel myself when I come back.'

She glanced up at him. His dark eyes were fixed on the road ahead and she could find no irony in his face. It wasn't fair, she thought childishly, he shouldn't say things like that when she was determined not to like him. She felt, for some odd reason, that there was a kind of armour in dislike. She had a strong feeling that she might need all the armour she could muster against this fantastic man who had so much star quality that he was almost a constellation in himself. 'Bear me out, Hugo,' he said now, appealing to the man behind them.

'I will that, Mr St Ewan,' came Hugo's placid voice from

the back. 'We're all good Cornishmen here, you'll find, Miss Warrington.'

'There you are, you see, Kate. Convinced now?'

His first use of her christian name, spoken so easily in that deep, velvety voice, made her heart jolt ridiculously. She couldn't think why, for most men called their secretaries by their christian names. But how did he know what it was? He must have asked Mrs Ashbrook when he rang through yesterday to demand Kate's services. He must have had all this planned out, down to the last detail. It was just another angle on the way he worked. His present friendly approach to her was no doubt calculated too. It didn't mean a thing, she assured herself, her armour safely back in position.

Kate wasn't sure what she had been expecting the house to be like. Mrs Ashbrook had said the St Ewans were a very old family, and she had vaguely pictured a very old family house, romantic-looking with pointed gables and mullioned windows and lichen clinging to the roof. She couldn't have been more wrong. Certainly the entrance to the drive was in character—tall stone pillars topped by carved stone spheres the size of footballs—and the drive itself was long and winding between great tangles of rhododendrons and azaleas and hydrangeas. But when the house itself finally came into view it was a complete surprise. It was as modern as the morning, with picture windows set into a white façade. It was a beautiful house, no doubt; fabulously expensive, certainly. It seemed to have 'architect-designed' written all over it and its like could be seen hidden away behind the trees in any fashionable directors' belt in any big-city out-of-town suburb. It couldn't have been more than a few years old, and Kate wondered about the house it must have replaced. Was this Damian St Ewan's idea of a millionaire's residence?

He brought the Range Rover to a halt on the forecourt of the house and jumped down, coming round to offer a hand to Kate, but this time she managed to avoid the disturbing touch of his fingers curling round hers, and was out of the vehicle before he could reach her.

He looked down at her curiously. 'You *are* an independent little cuss, aren't you? Don't you like to be helped?'

Not if it means being touched by you, Kate thought, but she didn't have to make any reply, for at that moment a big black Labrador came padding round the side of the house and launched himself upon Damian St Ewan with little squeals of ecstatic delight that sounded rather like a concertina in inexpert hands. His master squatted down on his heels and the dog nuzzled him and pawed him, whimpering all the time, tail thumping against the wheel of the Range Rover. Kate looked on, judging that the immaculate brown suit and cream shirt was going to be a little the worse for wear after this welcome, but the dog's master didn't seem to mind. 'Good Jet, good old boy, you've missed me, haven't you, fellow?' He pummelled the animal's broad chest, ruffled his ears; indeed, it was difficult to decide which of them was enjoying the reunion most.

Hugo was lifting Kate's suitcase down from the car. 'He's given Marian quite a time since you've been away, squire,' he said. 'Wouldn't touch his food for the first twenty-four hours.'

Damian St Ewan straightened up and gave the dog's head a final caress.

'Talking of food,' he said, 'reminds me of breakfast. Have you had yours, Hugo?'

'At the crack of dawn. Marian rewarded me with mackerel because I got up early to meet your train.'

'Mackerel—superb! Do you suppose she'll have some left for us? Come along, Kate, we'll go and see. Do you like mackerel?'

'Very much,' said Kate politely.

He slanted her one of his devilish looks as he picked up her suitcase. 'As much as you like fillet steak?' His tone was teasing and she knew it was a reminder of last night and an invitation to her to be less formal. What had he said then? 'I was beginning to wonder if you were capable of

41

smiling, Miss Warrington.' Well, she wasn't going to unbend now just for his amusement. She was determined to be as formal as her position demanded. Her armour was firmly in place.

He seemed to be waiting for a response from her and when he got none he gave a little shrug and turned to Hugo. 'I suppose I'd better have the Daimler for Truro. Looks more fitting for a directors' meeting.'

'Right,' said Hugo. He jumped up into the driving seat of the Range Rover. 'Come on, tyke, you'd better stay with me.' The labrador had other ideas and turned pleading eyes on his master, who slapped him on his broad rump and ordered him forcefully to obey. Reluctantly he did so and Hugo reversed the vehicle and drove it to the side of the house. Damian St Ewan picked up Kate's suitcase and said with somewhat exaggerated courtesy, 'Shall we go in, then, Miss Warrington?'

The inside of the house was exactly as the outside had suggested—ultra-modern, luxurious, very much the type of house that a top executive might choose to live and entertain his friends in. It was designed in an open-plan, split-level style, so that there was a feeling of space and air as soon as you went in. There were acres of velvety carpet in a muted amethyst colour and the deep-cushioned bench sofas that were cleverly built in to alcoves and against the rise of the higher level were of jewel shades too: topaz and coral and creamy pearl. There was a dining table on the raised area, before the wide sliding windows that were open to disclose a breathtaking view of the garden with the moors beyond. It was a beautiful room, but to Kate it seemed oddly out of place in this wild Cornish country. Still, it was no business of hers, and if this was the kind of house Damian St Ewan liked, then good luck to him. It wasn't her idea of a home.

A door opened at the back somewhere and a young woman in a blue dress came over to them, smiling. 'Hullo, Damian, glad to see you back safe and sound. I heard the car.' She glanced towards Kate. 'Your breakfast's all ready for you. Hugo said you'd be starving after travelling.'

'We are—ravenous. Kate, this is Marian Harris, Hugo's wife, who looks after us both with true understanding of real Cornish appetites. Marian, Kate Warrington, who'll be staying with us. That okay? Sorry to give you rather short notice, but it was a'—he paused and Kate felt, rather than saw, the way his dark eyes lingered on her with amusement—'a sudden impulse, wasn't it, Kate?'

Marian Harris was a fair young woman, in her late twenties or early thirties, with soft hair and candid, very blue eyes. She greeted Kate pleasantly and said, 'I'll have your breakfast on the table in a jiffy. I've put a small table up there. Sit down—unless you'd rather go up to your room first, Miss Warrington?'

'I'll take Kate up, Marian, you press on with the mackerel,' said Damian St Ewan. 'The White Room? Come along, Kate, I'll get you installed and then we can eat.'

Kate followed him up the staircase, which rose from the back of the room, curving up to a gallery which enclosed three sides of the area below. The stairs themselves were open slats of some beautiful pale wood, and the handrail of the same wood, supported by slender steel banisters. It was all rather puzzling, Kate decided, that a millionaire should live in an establishment like this and yet that there should be such an air of complete informality. She had thought vaguely that his home would be somewhat intimidating, and bristling with chefs and stewards and chauffeurs and housemaids, for she knew that even in these democratic days you could get staff if you could afford to pay them.

'Here we are, then.' Damian St Ewan threw open a door leading off the gallery and took Kate into the most beautiful bedroom she had ever seen. She couldn't take it all in at once; she merely had an impression of softness and comfort and a whiteness like swansdown. Pale, satiny wood again, everything built-in; doors hiding recesses to be explored later; a wide picture window with a view over the moor.

'You'll be comfortable here?' Damian St Ewan dumped

her suitcase on the shaggy white rug beside the bed. He glanced round the room and grinned. 'Rather virginal, isn't it? But perhaps you will appreciate that, Miss Warrington.' He was laughing at her again.

'It's a very beautiful room, Mr St Ewan,' she said primly. 'I'm sure it will suit me very well.' And he could take that any way he liked.

To her amazement he burst out laughing. 'Point taken,' he said. 'Come down as soon as you're ready. I don't promise to wait breakfast if you're not down in three minutes.' And he went out and closed the door.

Kate was down in three minutes flat. A small round table was set in the window, in the raised part of the room, beside the large dining table. Damian St Ewan was already seated, with a stack of letters beside him on the table. He stood up immediately he saw her, and once again she was struck by the—what was the word?—the *charisma* of the man. The morning sunlight was pouring through the wide patio windows on to his gleaming black hair and brown face. He was so big and broad and powerful-looking that he seemed to dominate the whole of the space around him. In one way he was the same man she had first seen in that executive flat in London; in another way he seemed to have taken on a new dimension here. He seemed freer, possessed of a masculine vitality and zest that was almost frightening. She had to remind herself firmly that after all he was essentially a man of business, a money-orientated man, and because of that he had to possess a ruthlessness that he wasn't at present showing. She must on no account relax her guard or she would find herself actually liking the man.

As soon as Kate had taken her place at the table Marian appeared with grilled mackerel, plump and golden and meaty, with freshly baked rolls. There was toast and home-made marmalade, and coffee from a tall brown jug.

'Marian's a treasure,' Damian St Ewan remarked when they were alone again. 'I really don't know I'd get along without her and Hugo. Sometimes I get nightmares thinking they might decide to move on, but they seem happy enough as things are.'

He looked thoughtful, and Kate saw how organised his life must be in spite of the relaxed atmosphere in the house. A man at the top of a career as he was, dealing in millions of pounds as if they were pennies, needed exactly the kind of service that suited him best. Hugo and his wife fitted into the pattern, just as she herself apparently did.

'Have you any family living with you, Mr St Ewan?' She saw the quick, oddly surprised look he darted at her and added hastily, 'Not just idle curiosity on my part. I shall need to get my bearings.'

'Yes. Yes, of course. Well, the only people you are likely to encounter here at present, except me, are Hugo and Marian. They have their own part of the house, but usually we team up together for meals and so on. If they want to be on their own they just say so, and I do too. It seems to work quite well. I have a couple of married sisters, one living in Washington D.C. and the other in Scotland. Then there's my young brother Michael, a student of mining engineering. He's at present doing field work up in the north. And Jocelyn, the baby of the brood, in her final term at boarding school.' He frowned as if he had just discovered something. 'I'm afraid it will be rather quiet for you. I don't seem to have much time for a social life at present.'

'I'm here to work, Mr St Ewan,' Kate reminded him composedly.

He glanced enigmatically at her and picked up the top envelope from his pile of letters. 'Yes, so you are. Now, would you think me very rude if I opened my accumulation of mail while I'm finishing breakfast?'

The rest of the meal was passed in silence, which suited Kate very well. She had to adjust to the way things were evidently going to be while she was here. She had imagined herself having meals in her room, or possibly even with the staff, while Mr St Ewan lived in style elsewhere in the house, but she couldn't have been more wrong. She wasn't quite sure whether she was glad or not. Normally she would

45

have been glad. She wasn't an introvert by nature, in spite of what the girls at her flat imagined. They had come to that conclusion because she didn't seem to have any love life to discuss, as the rest of them did. The truth was that she hadn't any intention of getting herself involved with a London man. She knew very well what she wanted in a man—or rather, what she didn't want, and after Roger she had managed to keep clear of men who were career-minded in the world of big business. Here in Cornwall she would be delighted to meet new people, to make friends. She wasn't likely to count her new employer as a friend, but she had liked Marian and Hugo straight away. She decided that on the whole she was glad that the atmosphere seemed to promise something more easy-going than she had expected.

Presently Damian St Ewan tossed back his second cup of coffee and pushed back his chair. 'Finished? I'll show you the library before I go. I sometimes work there myself, but you can use it as you wish. It's pint-size and cosy.' He gave her a swift, ironic glance as they went across the big room together. 'You'll fit in there nicely, being pint-size and cosy yourself.'

That was pure sarcasm, because she wasn't pint-size, she was quite a tall girl, and she certainly hadn't shown any noticeable cosiness during their brief acquaintance. Kate didn't reply.

He sighed gustily. 'That was intended to be a humorous remark, but I can see it failed dismally. Tell me, Kate, are you always as cool and distant as you seem to be? Still suspicious of me? Still wondering if I've brought you down here with some dastardly scheme in mind?'

She looked up at him as they walked together towards a door at the far end of the room. Then, meeting those dark eyes that did such curious things to the regular beat of her pulse, she looked away again quickly. 'I know what you've brought me down here for,' she said. 'As a temporary secretary, of course.'

'Did I ever tell you that?'

'Well——' Rather wildly she cast her mind back, trying to

remember just what he had said in his London flat, but nothing emerged except a vivid memory of an enigmatic, utterly assured man who had bent her to his will as easily as he might have bent the stalk of a flower. 'Naturally, I took it for granted——' She stopped, swallowing hard.

'Don't panic, Kate,' he said, quietly mocking. 'I'm no Bluebeard and this is no Bluebeard's chamber.' He turned the door handle and led the way into the room that he had called the library. 'Here you are, make yourself at home. Now I must be away to my meeting. Marian will show you around and you can ask her for anything you need.'

'But isn't there——?' she began as he turned away. 'I mean, haven't you any work to leave with me to get on with?'

'You're a demon for work, aren't you? No, no work today. Your busy time will come next week when the Vestor chief arrives. Just find your way around. Amuse yourself. Renew that old love affair.'

Her eyes opened wide. 'What——?'

'With Cornwall,' he smiled as he went out of the room. A couple of minutes later she heard the soft purr of a powerful engine fade away down the drive.

Kate felt more at home in the library. It was indeed a small, cosy room and it had a friendly, lived-in look, in contrast to the rest of the house. There was a red turkey carpet on the floor, a well-worn leather settee and chairs, a massive mahogany desk. One wall was completely covered with books and there were several oil-paintings on the panelled walls. There were long french windows opening in the same direction as her bedroom window. Above the low shrubs immediately outside she saw moorland stretching away as far as eye could see, rising and dipping, dotted with granite outcrop, here and there purpled by clumps of heather. This was the real Cornwall that she remembered, and she stood beside the window for a long time, just looking at it and recalling, for a spice of extra pleasure, the horrid heat and smell and confusion of London in the rush hour. She told herself that she was incredibly lucky to be here, and she was going to enjoy it in spite of the unsettling, maddening man who was employing her.

She turned away reluctantly at last to examine the room where she was presumably going to work. There was a rather elderly typewriter on the desk. She found some paper in one of the drawers and tried it out. With a thorough clean-up it would produce reasonably good work, she decided. The desk drawers seemed to be crammed with oddments, cuttings, folders full of yellowing papers. There was no attempt at any orderly arrangement; it looked as if she were the first secretary to work here for some time, if not the first ever. She discounted her new employer's mysterious remark just before he left. Of course she was going to work as a secretary. If not, what possible reason could there be for bringing her down here? She wandered round the room, examined the books, which were nearly all heavy tomes on engineering, mining, minerals. There were one or two books about the history of Cornwall and Cornish tin mining. Some had fascinating photographs of underground workings, showing miners with hard hats with candles stuck on to them. She replaced the books, thinking that it would be interesting to read them later.

She looked at the paintings, all of them undoubtedly views of Cornwall, probably very good amateur work, she judged, although she was no expert. She paused at a painting of a house, in a narrow gold frame, and guessed straight away that this was the house that had orginally stood in place of the modern one that was here now. This was the kind of house that she had expected to see when she arrived; it fitted into its surroundings as the present one did not. It was beautiful, dignified, with its bays of Georgian windows and its wide, graceful arched doorway and important chimney stacks. In the foreground, tree shadows fell across a smooth lawn. All was fitting; it seemed to have grown into the landscape.

'Finding your way about, then?' Marian's voice broke in on her musings. She had come into the room without Kate hearing her.

Kate turned and smiled. 'I was just admiring this picture,' she said. 'Was this the original house, before this modern one was built?'

Marian nodded. 'Been in the family for hundreds of years.' She shook her head regretfully. 'Rather a shame, I think, to pull it down. Although you can understand Mr St Ewan wanting to get rid of it, I suppose. And this house is lovely, don't you think? So modern and convenient. Easy to run, too. I manage quite well with some help from the village each day.'

How could he be so insensitive? thought Kate. How could he pull down a beautiful old house like the one in the picture that had been in his family for generations, just to build a bright new place like this because it was up-to-the-minute? Roger had been like that too, she remembered; bored with her love of tradition, of old house and gardens; all for the new, the functional. 'You're too sentimental, Kate,' he'd told her. 'We can't live in the past.' She had tried to explain that she didn't want to live in the past; it was just that sometimes the world of the present seemed too hard, too ruthless, too geared to money and what it could buy. But Roger had laughed at her, and probably this St Ewan man would do the same if she dared to express her ideas to him.

'Have you been here long? Do you like it?' She spoke casually, just a question one girl might ask another, but Marian's blue eyes were suddenly guarded.

'Just over three years,' she said. 'We came here when the house was new. Yes, we like it very much. Hugo enjoys working for Mr St Ewan.' She flicked an imaginary speck of dust off the desk. Then she looked ruefully at Kate, who had perched on the arm of one of the leather chairs. 'Did I sound a bit lukewarm? It's just that sometimes I miss having a house of my very own. You see, Hugo had his own small business when we were married, supplying gear and instruments to the mining industry in Cornwall. We had a nice little house in Portreath. Then'—she shrugged— 'you know how it is, everything went wrong and Hugo had to borrow money, but it wasn't any use and in the end he had to give up. Mr St Ewan was very good to us then, because Hugo owed him a lot of money. He gave Hugo this job and we came to live here. I suppose we're lucky really,' she added, her blue eyes wistful.

'I understand how you must feel,' Kate said with sympathy. Marian Harris couldn't possibly know how well she understood. Damian St Ewan seemed to have come out of it all pretty well, she thought cynically, but then he always would come pretty well out of everything. She wondered just how generous his gesture had been, and how much had been pure self-interest.

'But I mustn't natter on to you, Miss Warrington,' Marian said, pushing back her soft fair hair. 'I've got a girl coming in to do some kitchen work and push the vacuum cleaner around and I'd better go and keep an eye on her. Is there anything I can do for you just now?'

'No, nothing, thanks. I'll come and look for you if there is. And please don't call me Miss Warrington. It's Kate. We're fellow employees here, after all.'

'Yes, of course,' Marian said quickly, but Kate had seen the surprised look in her soft blue eyes. More than surprised —puzzled.

Kate was puzzled too. Here was this mystery about her job again. What *had* Damian St Ewan told these people about her and why she was here? She would get that clear with him when he came back, she thought grimly. She didn't want any misunderstandings. 'I've come down here to work as Mr St Ewan's secretary,' she said. 'Perhaps he didn't explain that to you?'

Marian laughed rather confusedly. 'I didn't really know. He spoke to Hugo on the phone last night and Hugo said— oh, it's all too stupid.' She was rather pink. 'Well, anyway, let me know if I can help, won't you? And there'll be coffee going later on. I'll bring some in for you.'

'Where do you have yours?'

'In the kitchen, usually.'

'Then I'll join you if I may,' said Kate firmly. 'Do you

50

think it would be all right if I used the phone? I want to put a call through to Bristol.' She must let Nanny know where she was, and her letter wouldn't have arrived yet.

'I'm sure it would,' said Marian. She was still looking faintly embarrassed. She pushed the phone across the desk towards Kate and went out of the room, closing the door behind her.

Kate glanced at her watch and saw that it was a quarter to ten. Nanny would have had her breakfast by now and be engaged on doing her housework. She was very regular in her habits. Kate dialled the Bristol number and waited. She had herself had the telephone put in for Nanny when she went to London, and it had been a relief to know that Nanny could get in touch with her in case of emergencies. Not that there had been any, but Nanny was over sixty now and you never could be quite sure.

She gazed out of the window while she waited for the various clicks to go through their operation. She couldn't wait to get out on to that green and purple moorland. When she had spoken to Nanny, she decided, she would go out for a walk in the sunshine. She heard the brrh-brrh of the calling tone, and thought how pleased and surprised Nanny would be to hear her news; she had often talked to Nanny about Cornwall and how she longed to go back there. 'Some day when I've saved up enough I'll get a little cottage and we can go and live there and grow our own vegetables and it'll be super,' she promised, only half joking. 'You'd like to come, wouldn't you?' Nanny had laughed, knowing it was all just a castle in the air, as far as she was concerned, but Kate had seen the wistful look in the eyes that twinkled behind their spectacles.

She waited for a full two minutes before she replaced the receiver. A wrong number, probably. Nanny would never be out, this early in the day. Kate dialled again, waited again, but still there was no reply. Finally she pushed the telephone back, feeling rather worried, and sat looking at it. No need to panic, she told herself, there could be lots of reasons. Nanny might have decided to go out for the day, as the sun was shining; or she might have popped round to chat with a neighbour; she might even have decided to do her shopping before the heat of the afternoon. She stood up, frowning faintly. Then, impulsively, she dialled again, but again there was no reply. She would go out for her walk and try again when she came in, she decided, not quite able to still her slight feeling of unease.

She pushed open the french window and stepped out on to a wide path bordered by thick low-growing shrubs, which evidently led round to the front of the house. If she followed it she should be able to find a way out on to the moors beyond. She turned the corner just in time to see a dashing red sports car pull up outside the front door.

A girl got out, slammed the car door impetuously and ran across the forecourt. Kate had no inclination to meet a friend of the family just now and slowed her steps, but the girl had seen her and stopped. She was about eighteen, and a lovely shape. She wore a scarlet playsuit which covered very little of her silk-smooth brown curves. As Kate drew nearer she saw a shimmer of corn-gold hair, great swimming green eyes, and a mouth that could only be described as luscious, the whole effect adding up to something quite stunning in a sulky, creamy sort of way. But there was something in the way she just stood there waiting for Kate to come up to her, something vaguely disdainful, that put Kate on her guard.

However, one mustn't judge so easily, she told herself, and smiled pleasantly as she said, 'Good morning.'

The green eyes measured her. 'I'm Carole Oliver. Daddy told me that Damian had brought a girl back with him from London, so I thought I'd come and take a look.'

Kate recognised the type immediately. This was one of those spoilt rich, beautiful young women who thought it infinitely smart to be as bluntly rude as possible. When employed to a man the tactic was supposed to be provocative; to another girl it was frankly insolent.

Kate returned her stare. 'I'm Mr St Ewan's secretary.'

'Oh yes?' Again the insulting examination, taking in

Kate's casual pants and sweater, her dark hair falling round her face. She hadn't thought it necessary yet to set it into the neat, businesslike style she wore for work. 'You don't look much like a secretary. Did you think that one up yourself, or was it Damian's idea?'

It wasn't any use trying to meet a girl like this on her own ground, Kate knew. She had encountered the type before. 'You're mistaken, Miss Oliver,' she said quietly.

'Am I? Well, I hope I am, for your sake. I thought I ought to warn you from the start about a few things, in case you got the wrong idea. This isn't a run-up to taking over, you know, even if he has brought you home.'

'I'm afraid I *don't* know,' Kate said.

'Really? I should have thought I'd made it sufficiently clear. You don't *look* stupid.'

Kate's patience with this intolerable girl was beginning to wear thin. 'If you have anything to say to me, please say it.'

The girl lounged back against the portico of the front entrance, her scarlet playsuit making a vivid splash of colour against the white stone pillar. 'Certainly, as you've asked for it. To put it plainly, Damian St Ewan is my man. When we get around to it and both have the time to spare we intend to marry and continue the long and noble line of the St Ewans and the Olivers. My dear, you're wasting your time here.'

Kate wasn't inclined to start a slanging match, and anyway she guessed that nothing short of physical violence would penetrate the girl's sublime effrontery. 'Is that all?' she inquired coolly.

Carole Oliver's sea-green eyes narrowed. 'For the moment. Where is he?'

'Damian? I haven't an idea,' Kate said smoothly and with a tweak of astonishment that his christian name should come out so naturally. 'Perhaps you should keep a tighter rein on your fiancé and his whereabouts, Miss Oliver.' She turned and walked unhurriedly away across the forecourt

53

and out through a gap in the shrubs to where she could see the moor beckoning.

She pushed aside the overgrown bushes and stepped out on to the wide sage-green expanse of moorland, with the sunlight pouring down from a pale blue sky, turning the patches of heather to bright purple. She was breathing quickly and her knees felt weak. She had kept her end up, but she hated encounters like the one she just had. It had been so unnecessary too, and had put her in such a false position. It would have been quite simple to explain to Hugo and Marian, and again to this girl's father this morning, that she was here as secretary and not for any dubious reason.

It occurred to her suddenly that Damian St Ewan was doubtless in the habit of bringing girls down here and the thought made her even angrier, for some reason that she didn't stop to explain to herself. I don't care if he keeps a harem here, she told herself hotly, just so long as people don't take it for granted that I'm one of the inmates. Oh yes, Mr St Ewan, the moment you get back I'm going to know exactly where I stand, and you're going to tell me!

But for all her righteous wrath and determination, the prospect of challenging him, of meeting that compelling dark stare that could so quickly change to shrivelling dismissal if you tried to push him an inch along a way he didn't want to go, gave Kate a sinking feeling inside. She took a deep breath as she stepped out on to the springy turf of the moor. She would go for a good tramp and build up her courage.

She was going to need it.

CHAPTER FOUR

KATE walked for an hour. She would have liked to plunge into the very centre of the moorland, towards the two tors that rose up in the distance; it would have chimed in with her mood to take some violent exercise to work off the anger which that intolerable girl had roused in her. But it would have been plain stupid to venture alone into wild and unknown territory. Damian St Ewan would definitely not be amused if she had to be rescued from a bog or some such hazard that might exist in that lonely place. So instead she took care to keep in sight of the stone walls and the little grey cottages that here and there jutted out into the heathland.

She tramped along, the sun warm on her bare head, the breeze whipping up the colour into her cheeks and smelling, she could almost believe, of the sea, which couldn't be very far away. And soon the magic of Cornwall took over and her anger drained away. What did it matter that her employer was the type of man she liked least of all men, and that the girl who had just laid claim to him was in the same league—rich, arrogant, self-satisfied people? They were welcome to each other, and they would doubt suit each other very well. Nothing mattered beside the fact that she was here, really *here*, at last. Delight bubbled up inside her. Damian St Ewan had been right in calling it a love affair. He had meant it ironically, like so many of his remarks, but he had hit on the truth. This was her place; she was half Cornish and she was at home here.

She felt as if she could have walked on for ever, but eventually she remembered that Marian had mentioned coffee, and might be wondering where she had got to, so she turned off the moor and found her way to a narrow lane where the high banks on either side were lush with ferns and ivy and tiny yellow wild flowers which trailed over the rough granite blocks that protruded here and there from the overgrowth. Soon she came to a farmhouse and beyond that a cluster of cottages. There were children playing in the gardens. There was a cackling of hens and wonderful aromas of dinners cooking. One cottage, the one next-door to the farm, was empty, and Kate lingered in front of it, seeming to recognise her dream. Here was the garden at the side, a riot of marigolds and cornflowers and tall white daisies. Here was the apple tree, and beyond that a rough patch of earth that looked as if someone had planned to start a kitchen plot and changed his mind. And here was the cottage itself, small and grey and old, merging into the countryside as if it had grown there.

A woman in a pink pinafore came out of the side door of the farmhouse with a basket of laundry. Kate smiled and called, 'Good morning,' and the woman smiled back in a friendly way.

'I was wondering—do you happen to know if this cottage is for sale?' Kate asked her. It was a long shot, but she couldn't resist asking.

The woman put down her basket and came to the hedge. She was in her fifties, plump and cheerful-looking. 'We haven't heard yet if it's taken,' she said, with a soft West-Country burr in her voice. 'Mr Forbes only moved out a couple of weeks ago. He works over at the St Ewan quarry and he's just got married and gone to live in Camborne. But it wouldn't be for sale, I shouldn't think. This is all St Ewan land around here and they don't sell. You might in-quire up at the house if you're interested in renting.' She looked at Kate with some curiosity. Living so close, it was probably important to her who the next-door tenant would be.

Kate thanked her and walked on. She might have known, of course, that Damian St Ewan would own all the land round here. He would probably pull down those lovely old cottages and build modern little boxes in their places, she thought sourly, if it suited him financially.

Back at the house she was greeted by the whirr of a vacuum cleaner, wielded by a tall, lanky girl with a wide grin, whom Marian presented as Ida. Ida proved to be completely tongue-tied, but she stared at Kate with what seemed undue interest, from bright, knowing brown eyes. Here we go again, thought Kate. Now *she's* wondering exactly what I'm doing here, and drawing her own conclusions. It was really rather intolerable.

'We had our coffee earlier,' Marian told her. 'I've put some in a flask to keep hot for you.'

Kate sat down on one of the pine chairs with the soft leather-covered seats that helped to turn the kitchen into something that seemed to come straight out of a glossy magazine, and drank her coffee while she told Marian about her walk. Then she went upstairs to her beautiful white bedroom to change. It really *was* a beautiful bedroom, her first impression had been right. Behind pale wood doors that glided at a touch was everything the heart of woman could desire; fitted wardrobe, fitted dressing chest, mirrors that swivelled to any desired angle, an abundance of drawers, subtle concealed lighting. Behind the final door she opened there proved to be a shower-room, tiled in pale turquoise blue, with slim fish and fronds of seaweed patterned on the curtains. Kate couldn't resist it; she took a luxurious shower and dressed in a yellow cotton dress that had been a 'find' in the summer sales and which she hadn't yet worn. The breeze had tangled her hair and she brushed it down into its neat day style, twisting the damp ends round to make them lie flat against her neck. A light application of make-up and she was ready for the work that must surely come along soon. She would feel more settled when she knew what her duties were going to be, she thought, and resolved again to tackle Mr St Ewan about it when they met at lunch. She really couldn't tolerate any more misunderstandings about her position here.

But what was she going to say to him? She tried out several different approaches in her mind. 'Mr St Ewan, there's something you must tell me ...' *Must?* No, he wouldn't stand for that. 'Mr St Ewan, you've put me in a false position and I insist ...' No, too aggressive. 'Mr St

Ewan, I hope you won't mind my asking you . . .' Too door-mattish.

She gave it up. She would wait her opportunity and then play it by ear. Meanwhile, she would go down to the library and try to get Nanny on the phone once again. That at least would be one worry dispelled.

This time Nanny's voice replied and immediately Kate recognised that her uneasiness had been justified. 'Oh, Miss Kate, I'm so glad! I tried to telephone you at your flat yesterday evening, but one of the young ladies there said you were away in Cornwall. She said you hadn't left an address.'

Kate said quickly, 'Nanny, is there something wrong? Was that why you were trying to get in touch with me? I wrote to you, but you won't have had my letter yet. Is everything all right?'

Silence, except for a crackle on the line. 'Nanny—are you still there?'

'I'm here, Miss Kate,' Nanny said quietly. Then it all came out. It seemed that yesterday Nanny had had another visit from Mrs Gray's pleasant nephew and he had done quite a lot of persuasive talking, which had ended in asking Nanny to go with him to see his solicitor.

'He called for me this morning in his car, and took me in to Bristol to the solicitor's office. The solicitor was very nice too, but he explained about me not taking over the lease of the house after my sister Mary died, and he said he was very sorry but the lease had expired and his client —that's Mrs Gray's nephew, of course—wasn't in a position to renew it. So'—a pause, then Nanny finished in a suspiciously bright voice—'so I'll just have to find somewhere else, won't I? I'll manage quite all right, Miss Kate, you needn't bother yourself, especially as you're away. Mrs Gray's nephew says he knows of a nice bed-sitter he might be able to get for me.'

Kate simply couldn't listen to any more. 'Look, Nanny dear, I'm coming straight back to sort this out for you. Now, you just stay put until I get to you. I'll ring you back as soon as I've looked up trains and let you know when to expect me. And Nanny, *please* don't decide on anything until I arrive. Will you *promise* me?'

Nanny, sounding bewildered but touchingly pleased, promised, and Kate replaced the receiver. She didn't like it, she didn't like it at all. There was a very nasty taste about the whole matter, and the more she heard about Mrs Gray's pleasant nephew the more unpleasant he sounded. However 'nice' these men of business were being to Nanny, the fact remained that they were obviously bent on getting her out of her house. A bedsitter, after living in her own little home! Having to share a bathroom and probably a kitchen as well! Kate knew Nanny and her fastidious ways well enough to know that she would hate it. 'Over my dead body!' she said aloud, giving full vent to her indignation and disgust.

She was suddenly aware that someone else was in the room, and she spun round in her chair beside the desk to see Damian St Ewan standing in the doorway, large and immaculately groomed as usual, and watching her with a gleam of amusement in his dark eyes.

'You sound in an extremely dangerous mood, Kate.'

She jumped up and faced him. No need now to think up a tactful approach, the situation had changed. And at this moment he seemed to her like the enemy—the perfect example of the man of business to whom money, and the making of it, is the only consideration. 'Mr St Ewan, I'm sorry if it inconveniences you, but I'm afraid I shan't be able to stay after all. Something very important has come along that makes it absolutely essential for me to leave straight away, as soon as I can get a train to Bristol.'

He sauntered into the room, eyeing her calmly. 'There's someone ill? Dying?' he inquired.

'No, not that, but——'

'Good. Anything less dire can no doubt be coped with. Suppose we discuss this over lunch? Marian has put it all ready for us, and problems have a habit of becoming less insoluble after a good meal. Come along.' He put a hand

59

firmly on her shoulder and propelled her towards the door. The touch of his hand, hard and warm through the thin cotton of her dress, made her feel suddenly weak. For a treacherous moment she wanted to move close to him, to rest against the strength of his body. She drew away from him quickly and walked on ahead. How feeble of her—just because she had been upset about Nanny there was no need to turn to the first man who came along, especially a man like this one, who would hardly be interested in anything as remote from his own important concerns as an old lady's housing problem.

Lunch was set on the table by the wide window that looked over the garden. 'Marian's having hers with the new girl; she says she wants to keep an eye on her,' Damian St Ewan observed, as they sat down. 'This looks delicious, don't you think?'

'This' was an eye-catching lobster salad, which at any other time would have made Kate's mouth water, but just now her mind was on other things. 'Yes, very,' she said, helping herself absently.

Her companion sighed in a long-suffering way. 'I can see you're not going to enjoy Marian's masterpiece until you've unburdened yourself,' he said, 'so, out with it. What's the problem, and why does it seem so urgent for you to walk out on me?'

Kate crumbled her roll nervously. 'It doesn't just *seem* urgent, it *is* urgent, and I'm afraid I must go. It—it's a family matter, and you wouldn't be interested in the details. It's all rather complicated.'

'Try me and see,' he said calmly.

She glanced over at him but the dark eyes were not mocking, or ironic. 'Well, it's about an elderly friend of my family, someone I'm very fond of, and who has been very good to me. She has a little house in the suburbs of Bristol, where she's lived for some years, since she retired.' Kate rubbed her forehead. 'It's all a bit involved, but what it boils down to is that the owner of the house has died and left it to her nephew. He wants to sell the house and he's doing his best to persuade my friend to agree to move out. And now she's just told me on the phone that the nephew's solicitor has got on to her and is saying that the lease has expired. I don't think she even knew there was a lease— the house was rented by her sister originally, and the sister died some years ago.'

He was looking keenly across the table at her. 'This nephew—he sounds like a fairly slick operator. You can't just turn people out on the streets these days.'

'No, of course not,' said Kate, 'but she's rather kind-hearted and I'm sure she'll let herself be persuaded— conned, if you like. She wouldn't know how the laws work about these things, anyway.'

'Would *you*?' he said abruptly.

A little taken aback, Kate admitted, 'Well, no, not really, but I suppose I could find out. Anyway, I could stop them moving her into some tatty little bed-sitter. That's what they're trying to do,' she added bitterly.

He was silent for a few moments, then he said, 'This needs consideration. Eat up your lunch, Kate, while I think.'

'But it wouldn't be any good——' she began.

He threw her a quelling glance. 'Do as you're told,' he said.

It didn't seem worth making a stand about. She could hardly leave for the station here and now, and anyway she had to admit that she would be grateful for his advice. As a landowner himself he would probably know about leases and things like that. Also, she suddenly realised that she was hungry and the lobster salad looked extremely inviting. They munched their way through it in silence and went on to the fresh peaches afterwards. Now and again Kate stole a glance at the dark, preoccupied face of the man opposite. This was a fascinating glimpse of a millionaire tycoon in action, dealing with a problem. But she couldn't see how he could come up with a solution to this one, in spite of his undoubted skill in manipulating people and events. A take-over bid involving astronomical sums of money would be more in his line. She bit into a luscious peach and waited.

Finally he lifted his head, and once again the impact of that black, glittering glance made her feel quite dizzy. 'This friend of yours,' he said. 'Is she one of those old ladies who is devoted to her home and would pine away if she had to live anywhere else?'

Kate shook her head. 'Oh no, she's not that type at all. She's a very sensible, practical old lady. I don't think she's all that keen on living in Bristol. It's just a matter of finding her somewhere else at a price that she can afford, and it's not going to be easy.' She rubbed her forehead again. 'I suppose, in a way, you can understand how the nephew is placed. It's probably hard to sell a house with—what do they call it?—a sitting tenant in it.'

His mouth firmed. 'Don't you know that in business matters you can't afford to let yourself see the opposition's point of view? A fine business woman you'd make!'

That touched Kate on a sensitive spot. 'The very last thing I'd want to be is a business woman. I loathe business and everything connected with it!' she burst out heatedly.

He looked at her with surprise. 'A funny job you've chosen, if you feel like that,' he said with his customary edge of irony. 'But don't let us get sidetracked. What I was about to suggest was that your friend should move down here. How would she feel about that, do you think?'

'Here?' Kate blinked stupidly. 'You mean——'

'I mean, I happen to have a cottage empty on the estate. One of my managers has been living there, waiting for his new house to be finished. He got married and moved out only a few weeks ago, and I haven't done anything about finding new tenants yet. What do you think—would your friend take to life in the country?'

She stared at him speechlessly.

'Well?' he said again, and now he glanced at his watch.

Kate pulled herself together. 'I'm sorry,' she said, 'but you rather took my breath away. It—it would be such a perfect solution. She's always hankered after the country. She only went to live in Bristol because her sister had this

62

house there, and then she just stayed on, when her sister died, and it's been her home ever since. But—yes, I'm nearly sure she would be absolutely delighted. I'd have to ask her, of course.' Her eyes were shining with excitement. 'I noticed an empty cottage this morning, in the lane coming up to the house. Near a big farmhouse. Would that be it?'

He nodded. 'That's the one.'

'Oh, I thought it looked super. Shall I phone now? I can't wait to see what she says.' Kate was nearly gibbering now, intoxicated by the idea as she began to realise all that this might mean. If Nanny rented the cottage then she, Kate, would have a home here too. She wouldn't have to go back to London. She could get a job, surely, in Penzance or Truro, and she could afford a little secondhand car—or even a motor scooter—to get backwards and forwards. To come home here every evening instead of to the flat in Hampstead!

She said, 'But what about the rent? I forgot that.'

He waved that away. 'Hugo looks after rents. But certainly less than she's paying in Bristol. And we could arrange a lifetime lease.'

Kate was on her feet now. She felt light, as if she could fly up in the air. 'It's—it's very kind of you,' she said awkwardly, remembering all the things she had been thinking about him.

He smiled faintly. 'It happens to be in my own interest to stop you hareing back to Bristol. Oh, by the way, tell your friend, Mrs——?'

'Miss,' said Kate, and grinned. 'She wouldn't thank you to call her Ms. Miss Bebb.'

'Good for her,' said Damian St Ewan, and grinned back. 'Well, tell Miss Bebb that if she's in favour of all this I'll ask my agent in Bristol to contact her tomorrow. He's a good friend of mine—name of Fogarty—and has a very understanding wife. Between them they'll arrange everything for her, and about the removal of her furniture and so on. You can get the cottage ready for her this end and she can take up residence as soon as she likes.'

Kate beamed at him. 'She has a cat called Monty,' she said irrelevantly, and ran back towards the library.

Damian St Ewan came in just as she finished telephoning and was replacing the receiver. He carried a tray of coffee. 'Marian's busy, so I brought it with me myself,' he said. 'Well, what's the verdict?'

Kate let out a breath. 'She's absolutely thrilled, and I am too. I can't really believe it yet, it's taken an enormous load off my mind.' She looked round at him as he came behind her to put the tray on the desk. 'I really don't know how to thank you, Mr St Ewan,' she said rather shyly.

He stood looking down at her with an expression in his dark eyes that made her pulse flutter. Then, deliberately, he put both hands on her shoulders and turned her round in her chair. 'You're a very pretty girl, Kate,' he said, 'and there's only one way a pretty girl can say thank you to a man.' He leaned down and kissed her mouth slowly and appreciatively. 'There,' he said as he straightened up again. 'Consider yourself out of debt. Now, write down Miss Bebb's address and phone number, and then pour me some coffee. I'll ring through to Frank Fogarty while I'm drinking it.' He glanced again at his watch while he was dialling. 'You can have a good look round the inside of the cottage this afternoon, Kate. Ask at the farm next door for the key and tell Mrs Norris I sent you.' He turned back to the phone. 'Hello. Oh, hullo, it's you, Frank. Damian here. Look, Frank, I've got a small job for you——'

Kate gulped her coffee, painfully conscious of the tumult inside her, while he organised the matter in hand. He was like a computer, she thought, with a baleful glance at the dark, masterful face of the man now totally concerned with what he was doing. Even his kiss had had a kind of calculated feeling about it. He had wanted to kiss her so he had kissed her, and that was that. By now he had no doubt forgotten all about it. It would never occur to him that she had been disturbed by the touch of his mouth on hers, as no man had ever disturbed her before.

She put down her cup, clattering it nervously on the

saucer. She must take a firm grip on herself. It would be utter disaster to let her emotions get involved with a man like this. She could be grateful to him because he had solved her problem—indeed, she *was* grateful—but it didn't prove anything, except that solving problems was something that a business tycoon did every other moment of the day, and no doubt in his sleep as well. He had decided that he wanted Kate here and he was, from self-interest, removing a small obstacle that threatened to come in the way. In five minutes he had coped with a problem that had worried Kate for years, but she couldn't allow herself to believe that he had acted out of kindness. If she did she might start liking the man, and that would be dangerous.

He finished his telephone call and stood up. 'That's all fixed, then. Frank and his missus will call on your Miss Bebb tomorrow and get things moving. And now I must get along. I've got to contact the engineers who've been doing the drilling at the mine. I can't say when I'll be back.' She could see that his mind was already on his business affairs as he added absently, 'Enjoy your house-hunting.'

'Yes, I will. And—thank you again, Mr St Ewan.'

'Damian,' he said, half-way to the door.

'Damian, then.' To her horror she felt her cheeks go warm. Mercifully he hadn't stopped to witness it.

A golden haze had settled over the countryside as Kate set out for the cottage, a little later. As she reached the turn in the drive there was a rustle in the rhododendron bushes and Jet, the labrador, emerged and stood looking at her.

'Hullo, boy.' Kate held out her hand for him to sniff and the big old dog took his time about deciding whether she was an acceptable addition to the household. Finally his tail began to twitch. 'Friends?' Kate suggested, fondling the massive black head, and was rewarded by the little squealing noise with which he had greeted his master this morning.

She found herself pleased out of all proportion to the event. Jet, at least, took her presence here for granted.

'Coming for a walk?' she said, walking on towards the lane. Jet seemed to ponder for a moment and then finally padded along after her.

The woman who opened the farmhouse door proved to be the same woman that Kate had spoken to this morning in the garden. The pink pinafore had gone and she was dressed in a sensible jumper and skirt, with her brown hair arranged in an old-fashioned plait round her head. It occurred to Kate that she would make a very desirable neighbour for Nanny, and when she introduced herself and explained her errand she was even more encouraged.

Mrs Norris beamed at her. 'Yes, of course you can have the key. Come along in, while I find it. I see you've got Jet with you.' She patted the dog's head. 'Lovely old dear, aren't you?' and to Kate, 'I've known him since he was a pup. He belonged to Mr St Ewan's mother, but I expect you know. Poor lady, she was devoted to him.' She heaved a sigh for somebody who had passed on, and led the way into the house, which was full of the smell of baking bread.

'Now, I think my husband put the key on the top shelf of the dresser. Ah yes, here it is. I'll walk over with you, Miss Warrington, and show you how to open the door. The lock's a bit tricky. Will you be thinking of renting the cottage for yourself?'

As they walked together to the cottage, Kate sketched in the circumstances. 'There now, that will be very nice.' Mrs Norris manipulated the key and pushed open the stout wooden front door of the cottage. 'I'll look forward to meeting your friend and making her welcome. There aren't many of us around here, but everyone's very friendly and there's always someone to give a lift into town for shopping and so on. I'm sure your friend will be very happy.' She beamed approvingly on Kate. 'You'll be all right now, and you can have a good look round on your own.'

Kate thanked her. 'Shall I bring you the key back?'

'Oh no, you keep it, Miss Warrington, and then you can come down whenever you like. You'll be staying up at the big house?'

66

'Yes, for a time. I'm doing some secretarial work for Mr St Ewan.'

'Oh yes, I see,' said the farmer's wife, and Kate thought wryly that it was a pleasant change when *somebody* did. 'I expect he's keeping you busy.' Mrs Norris lingered on the doorstep. 'Mr St Ewan's got a lot on his plate, as my husband says, what with the quarry and everything, and all the other companies he's interested in. And now I hear he may get Wheal Dora working again after all these years. It'd be a wonderful thing for the village if he did. Keep some of the young men here, p'raps. They all leave home, you know,' she added, shaking her head sadly. 'There's not enough work to go round. But with the mine open again, as well as the quarry, things might look up a bit.' She smiled hopefully. 'Ah well, we'll have to wait and see. Now I must get back to see to my bread in the oven.'

Kate thanked her for her help and went thoughtfully into the cottage. She hadn't considered the mine business as something that would bring more work and prosperity to what was an area of the county that would gradually run down without it. She had thought of it as a new toy for a very rich man who already was running huge concerns which must bring him in more money than he could possibly need. Perhaps he was more human than she had allowed herself to believe. She would have to wait until the actual work began before she made up her mind whether he just enjoyed manipulating things and people, or whether there was a more admirable side to him after all.

Inside, the cottage was a little gem. Kate explored it inch by inch while Jet snoozed under the fuchsia bush that dripped its crimson pendants beside the front door. There was a long, sunny parlour with the original wooden ceiling beams and deep-set windows; two bedrooms above, with built-in cupboards and dressing tables. Downstairs, at the back, was an extension consisting of kitchen, lobby and bathroom, with what she supposed was a utility room for washing and storage. The modernising had been done unobtrusively and with an eye to retaining the cottage's personality. She was sure that Nanny would love it, and she would love it too. She sat for a while on one of the low window-ledges and began to decide where all the familiar things would go, her head teeming with happy plans.

As she strolled back up the lane, the old dog padding along behind and panting in the heat, the golden haze persisted. There wasn't a cloud in the pale blue of the sky, and the far horizon across the stretch of moorland was misty with heat. The golden haze seemed to be inside Kate as well as out. It wasn't often, she thought, that a dream took form and became reality. She would work like steam for Damian St Ewan, just because he had made it possible when it had seemed impossible. Whatever the nature of the job he needed her for, she would do it to the very best of her ability, she vowed, and she wouldn't allow her dislike of what the man stood for to show more than she could help. She might grow almost to like the man himself, even if she couldn't admire his captain-of-industry image. She had seen that in action the first time she went to his London flat to take letters, before he went to Canada, and very impressive it had been too. But here in the country she wouldn't have to be constantly reminded that he was very much a part of the wheeling-and-dealing of big business. By the time she got back to the house Kate was almost hugging herself with complacency about the way everything was turning out.

She strolled round the side and across the lawn towards the patio that ran the whole length of the back of the house, where she had earlier noticed chairs and loungers set out, and a wrought-iron table topped with a huge striped umbrella. Tea here would be lovely; she would find Marian and see if she agreed.

Jet was still lumbering along beside her, knocking against her legs in a slightly tipsy but friendly fashion. 'You've really accepted me, haven't you, Jet?' The thought was somehow comforting and she stopped to fondle his soft black ears as she came up to the terrace. It was then that she saw that one of the canvas loungers was already occupied. With his dark head against a blue and orange cushion and his long legs stretched out in front of him was Damian St Ewan.

He had heard her. 'Come and join me,' he called lazily. 'I've taken the rest of the afternoon off, it's too hot to work. Isn't it, Jet, old boy?' as the big dog flopped down beside him, panting, tongue lolling.

Kate sat in a woven basket chair at a discreet distance, for the suddenness of the encounter had given her the familiar breathless feeling in her chest. It was really ridiculous, the effect this man had on her. She had only to see him for her knees to feel weak and her breathing to go haywire. And the way he looked at this moment didn't help at all.

Cornwall seemed to have taken him over completely. The long legs that had disposed themselves so nonchalantly in their business-man's suiting in London were now encased in ancient blue jeans. The cream silk shirt had given place to a faded striped cotton one, its sleeves rolled up to disclose brown muscular arms, and open at the neck to show an old-fashioned gold locket on a slim chain, nestling against the dark hair of his chest.

He was looking hard at her under dark lashes, his eyes glittering slits of black in the sunlight. 'Also,' he said thoughtfully, 'I thought we might take the opportunity of having a talk together, to sort things out.'

She was alerted by something in his tone, but he merely went on to say, 'How was the cottage?'

'Oh, it's absolutely super,' she enthused, immediately off her guard. 'It's just exactly what I dreamed of, but never expected to find. I really am most awfully grateful. And Mrs Norris seems such a nice person—I'm sure she'll be a really good neighbour.'

He nodded. 'The Norrises are good folk. They've been tenants of ours for ages. Well, I'm glad that's fixed up and your mind's at rest about it, because there's something else I want to discuss with you, Kate.'

'About my job?' she inquired eagerly. 'I'll be glad to start work any time you like.'

'I hope so,' he said enigmatically. 'Now, this is the position. I had a phone call this morning from Canada. Warren Lindsay plans now to bring his visit forward and he'll be arriving here next Wednesday; that's five days off. He's bringing his daughter Madeleine with him and they'll stay about a week. This is where I'll need your help.'

She nodded. 'You'll want me to look after Miss Lindsay while her father is engaged in his business here?'

She saw his lips twitch. 'Something like that,' he agreed. Then he sat up and leaned forward in his chair, clasping his hands together loosely. 'I wonder if you realise, Kate, how much this Wheal Dora deal means to me? An enormous amount is involved.'

She thought wryly: I bet it's an enormous amount. Millions. But she merely said, 'I'm sure it's very important to you. I read in the paper that you were hoping to raise a great deal of money.'

'I'm not looking for a loan,' he said. 'It's a matter of a partnership with Vestor's of Canada. Working in close co-operation for years to come. That's why this visit has got to go right on all levels.'

She nodded. 'I see.'

'I don't think you do,' he said dryly. 'But first of all perhaps I should explain exactly how you can help me.'

'Any way at all,' she said, thinking of Nanny and the cottage. 'You've helped me—now it's my turn. I don't mind how hard I work, and I really am quite versatile. We were trained in various other things besides shorthand and typing, you know.'

'I hardly think,' he said, watching her closely, 'that you were trained to do what I require of you. I think you rather jumped to conclusions when I asked you to come down here with me, Kate. I don't need a secretary, you know.'

She stared at him, her lips parting, her eyes wide. 'Then —then what do you need?'

'I need a fiancée,' he said with a grim little smile. 'And possibly, later on if the situation seems to require it, I shall need a wife.'

70

CHAPTER FIVE

KATE sat frozen in her chair. The sun was still hot on her head; the grass was still lush and green; the birds still twittered in high-summer lethargy, but she noticed none of it. Reality had left the situation and it had become totally fantastic. She had wondered about her job, but never in a thousand years could she have guessed what he intended it to be.

At last she moved and her chair creaked. She licked her dry lips. 'I'm sorry,' she said. 'I couldn't possibly.'

He sat very still, leaning forward a little, and the liquid dark eyes under their incredible lashes had a very strange effect on her. 'Couldn't—or wouldn't?'

'Well, both, I suppose.'

With a sinking feeling inside she saw his mouth tighten, but his voice was low and reasonable as he said, 'You really are rather inclined to make snap judgments, aren't you? There's nothing at all disreputable about what I'm asking you to do. Let me explain. You see, the difficulty is that Warren Lindsay plans to bring his daughter Madeleine with him. I met Madeleine when I was in Canada, this last week. In fact I couldn't avoid meeting her on every conceivable occasion. Without wishing to sound too lacking in modesty, I'm quite sure I know at least one reason why she wants to come to England with her father, and I'm resolved to ensure against any possible awkwardness in that direction. Which is why I need a fiancée. Understood?'

She stared at him. 'You mean that this Madeleine has fallen in love with you?'

'Love?' He grimaced. 'I wouldn't put it like that. Madeleine is quite a nice girl, but she's spoilt, and—like many rich men's daughters—she's a collector. She collects anything she fancies at the moment. She only has to say the word and Daddy provides the dollars. Unfortunately at the moment she happens to fancy me, and I'm definitely not for sale. But if there were any—er—unpleasantness, shall

71

we say, it might prejudice the success of the deal for me.'

'But surely that's absurd. I mean, business is something quite different.'

He gave her a slow, cynical look. 'You'd be surprised how the two overlap sometimes, and I can't risk it. There's a great deal involved here, Kate. Starting up a mine is a colossal undertaking, especially in these days of new technology. It involves a staggering capital expenditure. So surely you see why I'd be glad to make it worth your while to take on the job. You could name your own terms.'

'Money?' Kate's lip curled. 'You're offering to pay me for doing a thing like that? For—for cheating? Oh no, Mr St Ewan, that may be the way you conduct business, but it's not for me, thank you.' The sheer arrogance of the man! He'd been planning this from the first moment he suggested bringing her down here—even before that, from the moment he rang Mrs Ashbrook. Anger was mixed with some other emotion—disappointment, perhaps. She had been beginning to wonder if, after all, she might come to like and admire Damian St Ewan. But now . . . 'I think it's absolutely horrible,' she finished hotly.

He didn't look particularly put out. 'And yet only a minute or so ago you were offering to help me—"in any way at all", I think your words were. The frailty of women!' He smiled in a way that sent a shiver down her back.

'I did want to help you, but I didn't know you'd merely been—been manipulating me all the time. You'd got the whole thing worked out from the very beginning. You thought you could get me to do anything you wanted.' Her voice rose indignantly. 'Why couldn't you have been straightforward with me from the start? Why couldn't you have told me what the job involved?'

'Told you?' He smiled briefly. 'What a fine reception *that* would have got from you! Why, you behaved like a scalded kitten when you even imagined that my intentions might be less than purely orthodox. Good heavens, girl, if I'd told you what I was about you'd have scratched my eyes out. So I had to pin my hopes on being able to bring you round to my way of thinking when you found yourself in Cornwall, where you said you wanted to be. I thought I was doing fairly well until the Lindsays decided to bring forward the date of their arrival.'

'You were softening me up,' she said bitterly. 'All that stuff about having my time to myself, enjoying being in Cornwall! And the cottage ...' She broke off, staring at him in horror as the full meaning of all this dawned on her. 'You'd back down over the cottage, if I didn't agree to do what you want? You'd go as far as blackmail?'

'You have a pretty choice of words, Miss Warrington.' He leaned his head against the cushion again, studying her face, unperturbed. 'But if you stopped being all noble and wronged, and let your intelligence take over for a moment, you might ask yourself how could it have been blackmail, as you so prettily express it. I wasn't to know you needed a cottage so badly, was I? No, it was just gambler's luck to be dealt the ace of trumps. And the cottage is a splendid bargaining point, don't you agree?'

'Oh!' she gasped. Tears of frustration stung her eyes. 'Oh, you're hateful. Insufferable!'

He grinned. 'Quite a promising start for our engagement. They tell me it's always a good sign for the future, to begin with a little good honest aversion.' The grin disappeared. 'Now, suppose we get down to considering this thing calmly together?'

'There isn't anything to consider. I've told you—*no*! It's utterly dishonest and I can't do it.' There was another reason too, lurking in the recesses of her mind, but she couldn't put a name to it.

Damian leaned forward again. 'Look, Kate,' he said in a more serious tone than she had heard him use before. 'I can see this has been a bit of a shock to you, but I assure you that there really isn't anything dishonest about it, if you take all the circumstances into consideration. I'm simply offering you a job, a slightly way-out job it's true, but just a job. All you'd have to do would simply be there when the Lindsays come. You'd wear my ring, beam at me sweetly now and again. If you tried very hard you might even manage to look as if you were in love with me.' He smiled wryly and Kate wondered just how many girls *were* in love with him.

'That's another thing,' she broke in. 'Why choose me for the job? There must be lots of girls you know who'd enjoy it? Why not—Carole Oliver, for instance?'

His head jerked up. 'What do you know about Carole Oliver?'

'About as much as I want to.' Kate wrinkled her nose fastidiously. 'She came here this morning—to inspect me, she said.'

'The devil she did! I'm sorry about that, Kate. Knowing my Carole, I can imagine. She has quite a temperament. But if you've already met her then you can appreciate why I couldn't afford to get involved there just now.'

'Afford?' Her eyebrows went up.

'Afford the time,' he amended dryly. 'But I haven't answered your question, have I? Why did I pick on you? Firstly, I wanted to put the thing on a business footing. I didn't want to involve a girl I knew already—a friend. That might lead to all sorts of complications, and I'm far too busy just now to indulge in amorous entanglements. I thought of you partly because you'd told me you were keen to go to Cornwall, and I thought that would give me an advantage, and partly because Mrs Ashbrook spoke highly of you the first time you came, so I was convinced you wouldn't let me down if you once undertook the job. And lastly, my dear Kate'—his glance passed over her slowly as she sat there very straight in her crisp yellow dress, with her satin-dark hair clinging round her sensitive small face —'lastly, if you will forgive my being personal, I'm sure that my family would accept you without question as the kind of girl I'd choose to be my wife, if I ever decided to marry.'

She flushed. 'Flattery will get you nowhere, Mr St Ewan, and I can't really believe your family would expect you to choose to marry a little nobody from a typing bureau.'

74

He grinned suddenly. 'They might, at that. At any rate I've made no secret of my opinion of the other kind—of rich men's daughters.'

'Which is——?'

'That they're mostly spoilt brats,' he said. 'Carole Oliver is a good sample of the breed. She's a brat if ever there was one, though quite an intriguing one, I have to admit,' he added thoughtfully. 'Anyway, there's no question of my marrying anyone in the near future. As I said, I've got a lot on my plate and I'm going to be far too busy to play the romantic lover. So you see, it would just be a temporary matter, as I said.'

'How temporary?' asked Kate. All sorts of thoughts were chasing each other round in her mind, the principal one being that she couldn't bear it if the offer of the cottage fell through now.

'Until Vestors have signed on the dotted line. When Warren Lindsay gets back with his report it shouldn't take them long to make up their minds. Say two months from now for the whole matter to be tied up. Could you put up with me for that long, Kate?'

'And if I refuse—would you really back down about the cottage?' she said slowly.

His look gave her the answer. She saw in his face all the ruthlessness of a man who has set his heart on something and wouldn't let a little matter of conscience stand in his way. 'If someone deals me the ace of trumps I'd be a fool not to play it, wouldn't you think?'

She looked straight at him, at the strong, clever face, the firm line of his mouth, the penetrating dark eyes that searched her own so confidently, and she thought of the utter impossibility of disappointing Nancy at this stage.

She shrugged. 'Then I don't have much choice, do I?'

He smiled. 'Not really.'

'But,' said Kate, 'there's one thing I must get clear. What did you mean about possibly needing a wife?'

His smile broadened, but he sat quite motionless. He

looked, thought Kate extravagantly, like a tiger about to pounce on its helpless prey.

'Oh, that! We can forget about that for the moment.'

'We can forget about it for good,' she said firmly. 'If *you* wouldn't be favourably inclined towards marrying a rich man's daughter, then I would never in a thousand years agree to marry a millionaire tycoon.'

He laughed aloud, very pleased with himself now he had won, she thought. 'Is that how you see me, Kate?'

'Well, you are, aren't you?'

'I don't care much for the way it sounds. Millionaire tycoon! It has a sort of unpleasant ring to it. But why are you so allergic to big money and rich men, Kate? You must be unique.'

She shrugged. She had no intention of telling him her life story. 'I suppose it's just the way I'm made. Everyone has aversions.'

'And prejudices?' He looked keenly at her. She met his glance and slid away from it. 'If you like,' she said carelessly.

There was a silence. She could feel his eyes on her and wished she could meet them easily, nonchalantly, but she knew very well that she couldn't. When she considered the immediate future there were odd little tremors running up and down inside her and she had an awful feeling that she might begin to giggle hysterically. My dear, sweet Nanny, what have I let myself in for in your interest?

At last he spoke. 'That's settled, then. No wedding. Now, we have until the Lindsays arrive next Wednesday to do our courting.' He felt in an inside pocket of the jacket that hung on the back of his chair and pulled out a small leather box. 'I took the precaution of stopping on my way from Heathrow to provide myself with this. I hope it fits—if not we can get it adjusted locally, no doubt.'

So he had even remembered to buy a ring! 'You were very sure, weren't you?' she said, almost wonderingly.

'When you set your heart on something,' he said, and his eyes were not on her, but fixed on the far distance, away beyond the limits of the garden, 'you don't allow yourself to contemplate anything but success.' He flicked open the box. 'Try it for size.'

Kate put the ring on her engagement finger, glad that he hadn't offered to do so himself. That would have made the whole situation so much more false. It was a magnificent ring, of course, a huge, single diamond in a delicate gold setting that was modern without being quirky. In the sunlight it glittered and sparkled with rainbow brilliance.

'Do you like it?' he asked seriously. 'I'll get it changed if you don't.'

'Of course I like it,' she said, almost impatiently. 'Who wouldn't like it? It's a superb ring.' She held up her hand and gazed at the beautiful thing. It was impossible not to think of the last time a ring had gleamed on her engagement finger—Roger's ring. That hadn't been diamonds, it had been a Victorian ring, a pretty posy affair in pearls and emeralds. Kate had tried her best to love it, but somehow the thought that some other woman had worn it first was, for her, a kind of barrier. She wondered if he had kept it after she had handed it back to him on that ghastly interview after her father's funeral. Perhaps some other girl was wearing it now. It didn't hurt any more. All the pain was in the past and the only part of it that remained was the lesson she had learned then. Next time, she had thought, if there is a next time, it will be real and true and lasting. And now she had a ring on her finger again, and it didn't mean any of those things. It was funny, if you could see the joke.

Damian St Ewan was sitting watching her. 'You *do* like it?' She wondered why he was so concerned that she should be pleased, but perhaps that was merely because he made a habit of tying up all the details of whatever he undertook.

'Yes, I like it very much,' she assured him. 'Better than . . .' She stopped. That had been a bad slip, but perhaps he wouldn't notice it.

Vain hope—he missed nothing. 'Better than . . .?' he queried.

It was easier to tell the truth than to try a cover-up; he

wouldn't be deceived, anyway, nor would he be interested in her past love life. 'Better than my last engagement ring,' she said without emotion, and added, 'It was three years ago. It didn't work out.'

'Tough!' He was equally unemotional about it. Then he smiled. 'Well, at least no hearts are in danger of fracture this time.'

'I should hope not indeed.' She was pleased to notice that her voice sounded more confident now. She was just beginning to get accustomed to the idea that the relationship between the two of them had changed completely. She was working on a job, certainly, but it would no longer be a job where she deferred to her employer. As his fiancée she would meet him on equal terms, and if she were dependent on him to keep his word about Nanny's cottage, then he was equally dependent on her for the working out of this plan of his. The idea appealed to her sense of justice.

He got to his feet. 'That's settled, then. We can cope with details as they crop up. We might as well start by telling Marian our glad news.'

She didn't move. She said, 'That's another thing—what did you say to Hugo about me when you rang up from London last night? Marian looked rather strange when I mentioned I was your secretary.'

He laughed aloud. 'I expect she did. I told them that I was bringing a girl back home with me and that we were just about to get engaged, but that we didn't intend to announce it for a day or two.'

She gasped. 'You're incredible! Utterly incredible! How could you possibly know then that I'd agree to this—this crazy plan?'

Damian stood smiling down at her, thumbs resting loosely on the pockets of his jeans, feet apart, the very image of self-assurance. 'I just knew,' he said, and his dark eyes were narrowed, challenging her to deny it.

There wasn't any reply to such arrogance and Kate didn't try to think of one. She sat silently in the basket chair, ignoring the temptation to engage in a battle of words which she knew she would lose.

He held out both hands. 'Come on,' he urged. 'Marian's been making some of her super little iced cakes for tea.' When Kate didn't move he reached down, gripped her wrists and lifted her to her feet in front of him. She tried to disengage herself, but he held her more firmly, and although he was still smiling there was more than a hint of authority in his tone as he said, 'Don't pull away from me, Kate. We're engaged—remember? You'll have to get used to letting me touch you, even though you do hate millionaire tycoons.' He bent his head and kissed her lightly but unhurriedly. 'There, that wasn't so bad, was it?'

She swallowed convulsively and fixed her gaze on his chest where his shirt fell open to disclose the gold locket. Her heart was thudding hard and she was wondering if she would ever get used to the devastating physical reaction he aroused in her. It was so—so humiliating to feel like this about a man whom in every other way she disliked. Each new thing she found out about him increased her contempt for him and the things he stood for, and yet he only had to look at her, to touch her, for her treacherous body to respond as if to a powerful drug. And now they were 'engaged' he would have the right to touch her whenever he liked, to kiss her, to—— Her mind balked. 'No!' she said.

She didn't realise that she had spoken the word aloud until he asked, his mouth humorous, 'Was that a reply to my question, or were you making some important decision of your own?'

Her cheeks flamed. 'It was— I was——'

'I know what you were thinking,' he said quite gently. 'And the answer is, Kate, that I'm not going to take advantage of the situation we're in. You've been engaged before, so you know what I'm talking about, don't you?'

She stared down at the stone paving of the patio. 'Yes, I suppose so,' she admitted in a muffled voice. 'But it wasn't like that before, anyway.'

'Wasn't it?' He regarded her quizzically. 'Well, I haven't the right to ask any questions about that either. I can only assure you that I won't do anything that you object to. Satisfied?'

She nodded. Why should he want to make love to her, anyway? This absurd 'engagement' was a business arrangement only, he'd made that abundantly clear. If he had been attracted to her he would never have chosen her to play the part, would he? He hadn't time to get involved in any romantic situations. He was far too selfishly concerned with his main objective—making money. She reminded herself of that as they turned towards the house, his arm loosely around her. Then a light voice called from behind them and his arm dropped away. Carole Oliver was running over the lawn from the direction of the front drive, her silver-gilt hair flying in the sunshine.

'Damian! I've found you at last. I've tried everywhere— I even phoned Truro and they told me you'd left for home.'

She ran up the terrace steps and put her arms round his neck, laying her smooth cheek against his brown one. 'Welcome home, darling. It's been hell without you.'

He was smiling. 'What a welcome! You and Jet leave me quite breathless.'

Carole frowned in pretty perplexity. 'Jet?' She looked down at the big black dog, snoozing beside the chair his master had just left.

'He was almost embarrassingly pleased to see me back too,' Damian explained. He tweaked a strand of her pale hair. 'You're looking extremely alluring this afternoon, Carole.'

Alluring was the word, Kate thought. She had changed the scarlet playsuit she was wearing this morning for wide white pants and a clinging, revealing, sea-green top that matched her eyes almost exactly. She looked like a lovely, sulky mermaid.

She linked her arm through Damian's and cuddled herself against him. Kate wondered exactly what was the relationship between these two, and how far the girl's claims

80

of this morning were justified. *Did* Damian intend to marry her 'when they both had the time' as she had said in that throw-away tone? At the moment he was treating her rather like a favourite younger sister, but that would no doubt be his attitude in the circumstances.

She gave his arm a little tug. 'Darling, I've got a heavenly new car to show you. Come and see.'

He shook his head. 'Sorry, Carole, no time now.'

'Oh, but you *must*,' she wheedled. Her sea-green eyes flickered over Kate, acknowledging her presence for the first time. 'Send your secretary away to do some typing or something. Then let you and me have a lovely drive in my lovely new car.' She was stroking his bare arm, her finger tips kneading his flesh like a kitten's paw.

Not a mermaid, Kate decided, a siren. One of those false, fabulous creatures who sit on rocks, singing and combing their hair, and luring susceptible sailors to their death under the waves.

But Damian St Ewan couldn't be considered susceptible and he no doubt had his own way with sirens as with everything else. Still smiling, but very firm, he removed himself from the girl's grasp. 'Sorry, Carole, you've got things a bit wrong. Kate isn't my secretary, she's the girl I'm going to marry. We've only just this minute made up our minds. You can be the first to congratulate us.'

The sea-green eyes dilated; for a moment the lovely animated face was quite blank. Then Carole laughed gaily. 'Darling Damian, you do love trying to shock people, don't you? But I just can't buy that one.'

'I'm not joking, Carole. This is for real, isn't it, sweetheart?' He reached out and drew Kate against him, looking down at her with great tenderness in his dark eyes. It was utterly convincing, thought Kate, feeling quite shattered, but of course he was a superb actor, just as he was a superb everything else. 'Isn't it, Kate?' His arm tightened, reminding her of her own part in the play.

'For real,' she echoed, and smiled brilliantly up at him,

wishing she had had just a little more time to adjust to this impossible situation.

Carole gave Kate a studiedly insulting inspection from head to foot. 'Her? You're not engaged to *her*? You couldn't be!' Just for a moment she looked as if she might burst into tears, the angry tears of a spoilt child deprived of a coveted toy. Then her face changed and she didn't look like a child at all. Her eyes narrowed craftily. 'I don't believe it,' she said, 'you're up to one of your games, Damian. It's all as phoney as hell, and you can't take me in. But I can see you mean to stick to your story for the moment.' She met his smiling gaze defiantly. 'When you've finished the game you can get in touch,' she said with an attempt at indifference.

She turned abruptly and walked back the way she had come. She would have been pathetic, Kate thought, if there had been anything likeable about her at all. But if there was, it wasn't apparent. With a little pang she suddenly remembered how she had once believed that everybody was good at heart and that when people seemed objectionable you only had to look a bit deeper to find the real, warm, well-meaning person trying to get out. It was sad that she couldn't believe that any more. Perhaps that was what growing up meant.

'Well, well, what a performance!' Damian replaced his arm around Kate's waist. 'Sorry about that. I told you she was a spoilt brat, didn't I? She'll get over it.'

'I wonder if she will,' Kate said slowly, falling into step beside him and trying not to notice the sensations that his hand on her waist were arousing in her. 'She left me in no doubt this morning that she considered you her property. In fact she warned me off. I think she took it for granted that you'd brought me here for—er—questionable purposes. She didn't seem at all convinced when I told her I was your secretary.'

She saw the flash of anger in his eyes. 'Sorry again, I seem to have put you in an embarrassing situation—quite unwittingly, I promise you.'

'Just a small detail you overlooked?' Her voice was guile-less; it was pleasant to be able to meet him on equal terms. 'I must say I got the impression that when *you* planned anything you never missed a trick.'

He stopped short and turned her round to face him. 'For that impudence I shall demand payment.' He lowered his head, drawing her close. 'I see Marian approaching, so let's put on a convincing act for her benefit.' And he kissed her again, this time more slowly and with considerable relish.

Marian came up to them as he stepped back. 'Do I inter-rupt something?' She came to a stop a little way from them, holding a tea tray in her hands, eyebrows raised expectantly as she looked from one to the other of them. She was quite obviously waiting to be let into a secret that she already knew.

Damian said, 'All right, Marian, it's a fair cop, as they say. Kate and I are engaged.' He took the tray from her and put it on the table under the striped umbrella.

Marian beamed at them. 'Oh, my goodness, I *am* pleased! I can highly recommend the wedded state. Lots and lots of happiness to you both. May I see your ring?' She examined it and pronounced it superb. Then she kissed Kate, who felt a hypocrite, for she was sure that Marian was a nice person, warm and sincere, and she hated to deceive her.

Damian seemed to have no such scruples. As Marian held out her hand and said, 'I think you're a lucky man,' he agreed happily and hugged her with all the exuberance of a delighted lover. Just how false can you be? Kate thought, with distaste.

Marian pushed back her soft fair hair, laughing, and said, 'I'll set the tea things out and then I'll be tactful and leave you two on your own. You'll have lots to discuss.'

Before Damian could say anything Kate had sat down and pulled up a chair for Marian. 'Of course you'll join us,' she said firmly. 'We'll have plenty of time to ourselves, won't we, darling?' She smiled radiantly up at Damian, and was gratified to see the way his eyebrows rose a frac-tion. If she'd got to play this game of his, then she might as well get some fun out of it. If he imagined he had selected a submissive little yes-girl to suit his purpose then he might be in for a surprise!

But if he had any qualms about what he had taken on he wasn't showing it. He lounged back in his cushioned garden chair drinking tea and eating iced cakes, the very picture of a man who has everything going his way.

'Um, delicious cakes, as usual, Marian,' he murmured appreciatively. 'You work too hard, feeding us. When are these new people due to arrive?'

'The Graysons? They're coming tomorrow morning.' Marian turned to Kate and said, 'Did Damian tell you that we've managed to engage a married couple to take over some of the work here?'

'About time too,' growled Damian. 'You do far too much yourself, Marian, you always have.'

'I enjoy it,' she said. 'I like being busy about a house. So far I've managed with girls in from the village to help,' she went on to explain to Kate, 'but that's getting rather dicey now because so many of them go to the coast for the summer season, to work in the hotels and cafés, and so on. It's livelier for them there. This couple are from Yorkshire, Kate, they're in their fifties and they have very good references. I hope you'll be satisfied with them, but of course you can arrange staff to suit yourself when you take over.' She glanced at Damian. 'But it's too soon to start talking about domestic plans, isn't it?'

'Much too soon,' he said comfortably. 'We're doing very nicely as we are. Is there any tea left?'

Marian took his cup and shrugged towards Kate. 'Isn't that like a man? It wouldn't occur to him that as mistress of Trestenak you'll have your own ideas as to how it should be run. I expect you'll want to change lots of things after you're married.' Her blue eyes took on a sudden bright shine, as if some exciting idea had just occurred to her, but she merely said, 'I suppose you haven't fixed anything yet?'

'Fixed?' Kate repeated. So many things seemed to have fixed since yesterday afternoon—none of them by her—

that she was beginning to feel like a very small fish that has accidentally swum into a torrential, rushing river. She glanced at the cause of all this, who was lying back contentedly, letting the sunshine pour down on to his dark face. He certainly didn't look very rushing or torrential at the moment, but Kate had a strong feeling that this lazy, relaxed manner of his was merely the calm that he cultivated so that the storm, when it came, should be more surgingly effective.

'Fixed the date you're going to get married,' Marian said.

Kate's eyes opened wide. 'Oh—oh no, not yet.' She cast a baleful look at Damian; he might at least help her out over things like this. He opened his eyes, grinned broadly, and to her discomfiture said, 'It can't be too soon for me, but I suppose women have to consider things like clothes.'

'Of course.' Kate seized on the subject of clothes as a safer topic. 'I'll need to buy some clothes straight away as I'm staying on to meet the Lindsays from Canada. You see,' she went on to explain to Marian, as Damian's eyes had closed again, 'I wasn't expecting to come back with Damian yesterday. It was all decided on the spur of the moment and I didn't have much time to think what I should need.' That, at least, was the plain truth. 'I expect I'll be able to get everything I want in Penzance or Truro, shall I?'

'Certainly you will,' Marian told her enthusiastically, 'and you've come to the right person for advice—I hope. I worked in the trade before I married Hugo.' She named a famous store with branches all over the country.

That began a dialogue about clothes. Kate pulled her chair closer to Marian's, asked interested questions, drew her out about her former job, about new materials, fashions, shops, anything that would fill in the time and keep the conversation out of awkward channels.

Presently Damian got to his feet. 'I'm obviously redundant at the moment,' he grinned, 'so I'll go and occupy myself with merely masculine pursuits and leave you two girls to discuss important matters. If anyone wants me I've gone back to Wheal Dora to have another try at contacting the engineers. See you both for dinner? Perhaps Marian could produce a small fatted calf for the occasion? You and Hugo will join us for the celebration, I hope?'

Marian looked doubtful. 'Of course, we'd love to. But are you sure we shouldn't be butting in?'

'Kate and I,' said Damian, 'look forward to having the rest of our lives together, as she just mentioned. Au revoir, my love.' He put a hand on her shoulder and kissed her just where her dark hair fell away from her temple. Then, with a salute to them both, he strolled away across the grass.

Marian looked after him, sighing. 'He *is* a sweetie. I can't tell you how happy I am for you both. He's always made a point that he intended to stay unattached and I was beginning to think he really meant it. This really has been a pleasant surprise.'

Kate bent over the teapot, pouring out third cups for both of them, trying to hide her pink cheeks. Her forehead tingled where Damian's mouth had rested on it and she was conscious that she was flushing abysmally. Well, at any rate *that* would look convincing, she thought crossly. A girl wildly in love would be expected to behave like a besotted teenager. But she was no longer a teenager, and she certainly wasn't in love, so it was nothing but a nuisance that her merely physical reactions should let her down all the time.

Marian took the cup of tea from her. 'Have you two known each other long, Kate?' Friendly, interested, not curious. And certainly not suspicious as Carole Oliver had been. Kate felt on firmer ground. 'Not long at all. In fact it's all been a bit of a surprise for me as well.' Too true it had!

Suddenly there was something she wanted to know and she didn't know quite how to ask. Then, meeting Marian's candid blue gaze, she decided that the straightforward question would be the best one. 'I suppose Damian's been wildly pursued by females? He's very attractive.' She tried to look convincingly rapturous.

Marian gave her a knowing look. 'Madly attractive,' she

agreed, 'and there have been several girls with their sights fixed on him since I've been here, but he's never shown the slightest inclination to link up with any of them permanently.'

'Not Carole Oliver?' Kate selected another cake carefully.

Marian looked thoughtful. 'Carole Oliver? She wants him, of course, that's quite obvious. And sometimes I've thought that he—but I don't know. Still, happily that's all in the past tense now,' she added cheerfully. 'She wouldn't have done for him at all.'

The conversation reverted to clothes again, but Kate's mind was not wholly on the subject. She kept seeing the lovely, sulky face and the smooth, seductive body of Carole Oliver; kept hearing that husky, challenging voice that said so confidently, 'When we both have time to spare we mean to get married.' She kept remembering, too, how Damian had looked at Carole when she had thrown that temperament just now. There was amusement, but there was something else too and she wasn't sure what. It might not suit him to be involved with Carole just at the moment, for she would certainly be a time-consuming luxury, as he had said. But when all this was over, when the important deal was clinched, when Kate herself had gone and this ridiculous charade was over, then——

Feeling unaccountably depressed by the track her thoughts were following, Kate firmly brought them back into the safer ways of clothes and shopping.

When they had finished tea Marian took Kate on a tour of the house. 'I'll just show you where all the rooms are and then you can find your way around.' The house was larger than it had appeared at first sight, perhaps because it was, quite evidently, the work of a brilliant architect. As well as the vast open-plan living room and the small library on the ground floor, there were extensive kitchen quarters, equipped with every gleaming modern appliance, and a games room with billiard table and pin-boards. Here there were tennis racquets, golf bags, water skis and other oddments and gear lying around in various stages of tidiness and untidiness.

'Mostly Michael's and Jocelyn's,' explained Marian. 'Damian never seems to get much time for sports, but perhaps now he'll make himself relax and not work quite so hard. You'll have to take him in hand, Kate, but I don't suppose you'll do much good with him—not even you—until this Wheal Dora affair is settled up. It's meant so much for so long—ever since his father died. But he'll have told you about that, of course.'

Kate smiled wryly as she followed the other girl up a back stairway to the first floor. What would Marian's reaction be if she said what was in her mind—that Damian had told her nothing, that she knew nothing about him at all, except that he was disgustingly rich, that he had an arrogant certainty that he would always get everything he wanted, that the idea of her 'taking him in hand' was something so unthinkable that it was almost ludicrous?

The stairs led to a small, compact, four-room flat, comfortably furnished as was the rest of the house. 'This is our own place, Hugo's and mine,' Marian told her, straightening the cushions on the settee and flicking an imaginary speck of dust off the table.

'Nice,' said Kate, looking around.

'Very nice,' Marian agreed. 'Damian had it all specially done for us when it was arranged that we should come to live here.' She hesitated, glanced at Kate, and added, 'I feel an ungrateful beast for being so thrilled and excited that we'll be able to move out soon.' At Kate's look of surprise she added, with a little smile, 'This house won't need two mistresses. When you and Damian are married that will free us to find a place of our own again. I was beginning to think we were stuck here for good. It's suited Damian so well to have us here, and neither of us would let him down, not for the world, because he was so awfully kind to us when things were bad. But now Hugo's out of debt at last and he has a good job that he loves, managing the quarry for Damian, and we could afford to start to buy our own house again.

There's something about a house of your own'—the blue eyes were dreamy—'it gives you a sort of pride, of confidence, don't you think? And I would so love to start a family.'

Kate nodded, feeling vastly uncomfortable. She wondered what Marian would feel like if she told her the truth. She only wished that she could; it was most unpleasant to think that you were allowing a nice person to live in a fool's paradise.

'Now I'll show you the bedrooms,' Marian said. There seemed to be a great many of them, all with their own bathroom or shower-room. 'These two are the ones that the Canadians will have,' said Marian, opening two adjoining doors. 'And this one at the end, I'd planned to give to the Graysons, the couple who are coming tomorrow. I thought that if they're satisfactory and seem like settling down they could have our flat when we move out. But of course that will be for you to sort out, Kate. Now I must go down and see about this celebration dinner. I'd arranged to have duckling tonight anyway, and that should be sufficiently festive if I dress up the orange sauce a bit, don't you think?' She laughed happily. 'Oh, it's all so exciting—the nicest thing that has happened for ages. Hugo will be thrilled when he knows what's been going on here while he's been at the quarry.'

With every word Kate was feeling guiltier and guiltier, though why she should do so she didn't quite know, for it was Damian who should bear the blame. It was a relief when Marian finally left her and went downstairs and she could escape to her own room. She swilled her hot cheeks and went over to the window, looking out and trying to recapture the pleasure she had felt at her first sight of the moor—was it only this morning? So much had happened since then that it seemed like days ago. But presently the sight of the rolling green landscape, so peaceful, so empty, began to have a soothing effect. What, she asked herself, was she worrying about? Compared with this time yesterday, when she had been on her way to Damian St Ewan's flat, everything was wonderful. She remembered how she had thought that it would need a fairy godmother to help her out of her difficulties, and now it looked as if the said fairy godmother had been lurking around unseen all the time. Almost by magic Nanny's house problem seemed to be solved, and she, Kate, was where she had longed to be, here in Cornwall.

Two wishes granted! But the best fairy godmother always gave you three wishes, didn't they? She would have to think up a third while the going was good. 'I wish,' she said aloud, smiling at her own fancy, 'that you would stay around for the next week or two, Fairy Godmother, and give me a spot of moral support and save me from making a fool of myself. Oh yes, and that you will make sure this idiotic engagement thing doesn't last a minute longer than absolutely necessary.'

And now, she thought, dragging herself away from the window and the view, she must pull herself together and select something to wear at this farce of a celebration this evening.

CHAPTER SIX

KATE slid back the door of the wardrobe and surveyed its contents with a rueful smile. On the long rail which would have accommodated a film star's outfit the four dresses and one summer coat looked pathetic. If she were going to carry off this charade of an engagement properly she must certainly go shopping very soon.

There was the matter of jewellery too, for all her jewellery had been sold after her father's financial crash. 'You don't have to sell your things,' he had demurred, grey-faced with shock and misery. But Kate had insisted. It would have seemed dishonest to keep them when all the shareholders in her father's business had a better claim. It kept her awake at night worrying about the people who were going to lose their money—perhaps their life savings if they were old and retired. So her jewellery had gone, together with her sports car and her mink wrap, and she hadn't really missed any of them. The bits and pieces of costume jewellery she had worn since then had come from a department store in Oxford Street. Some of them she had stuffed into her case at the last minute. She had chosen them and paid for them herself and she liked them; but they wouldn't look right on the future wife of Damian St Ewan.

Before she could decide which dress to wear tonight Marian tapped on the door and came in. 'Everything's well in hand cookingwise,' she said, 'and Ida's offered to stay on this evening to wait at table and tackle the clearing up afterwards. She's done some hotel work so she should be able to cope. I thought we'd get together for a drink about half past seven and have dinner at eight. Is that all right with you? I shall instruct the men it's an "occasion", otherwise Hugo is likely to insist on coming in to dinner in sweater and slacks.' She grinned tolerantly.

If it was going to be a dress-up evening, then Kate's mind was made up for her. She took out the Liberty silk dress and laid it across the bed, and Marian cooed with professional approval, touching the supple silk, patterned in yellow and burnt orange and mint green, splashed against an ivory background. 'It's an absolute pet,' she breathed. 'Couturier, of course. You can always tell by the finish.' She was admiring the almost invisible stitching inside the draped neckline.

Kate admitted it, thinking that it wouldn't surprise Marian that Damian should choose a girl who could afford to buy couturier clothes. It might surprise *him* more than a little, though, only she had no intention of telling him more than she need about herself.

When Marian had gone Kate looked at her watch and decided that she had time to write to Nanny before she need start to dress. She sat down at the writing desk near the window and began on a detailed description of the cottage and its charms, its convenience, the garden, the helpful neighbours. As she wrote she began to feel more reconciled to the part she had agreed to play for the next few weeks. She said nothing to Nanny about any engagement, false or otherwise, and merely referred to Damian as 'Mr St Ewan, the man I've come here to work for.' She nibbled the end of her Biro, gazing out of the window and thinking what an understatement *that* was. Her thoughts became so complicated that she had to drag herself back to her letter. 'I shall get the cottage thoroughly cleaned and aired and all ready for you,' she wrote. 'Let me know if the Fogartys are giving you all the help you need and if there is anything more I can do. I really intended to come to Bristol myself, as I said at first, but Mr St Ewan needs me here and he seemed to think that Mr and Mrs Fogarty would do anything you wanted . . .'

By the time the letter was finished it was nearly seven o'clock. She took a quick shower, did her make-up carefully, brushing her dark hair loosely round her face before she stepped into the cool, caressing folds of the Liberty dress. Looking at herself in the mirror she decided that Marian was right, it was a pet of a dress. The style was one that didn't date, fortunately, and it moulded her figure perfectly, swinging out from the hips and falling in soft flutes to below her ankles. She didn't think anyone would suspect that it had hung unworn in her wardrobe for nearly three years.

Her costume jewellery was in a small box on the dressing table and she looked inside and closed it again. Nothing there could be worn at the same time as this magnificent ring that felt so strange upon her third finger. She held up her hand and looked at it and the facets of the beautiful stone shimmered in the evening light. If only it had all been real and not make-believe, she thought, if Damian St Ewan had been an ordinary man, a man she could have loved . . .

But he wasn't, he was a hard business man who had struck a hard bargain with her, and she mustn't forget it. She would keep her side of the bargain as well as she could. She would act the loving fiancée to him and make it as convincing as she knew how—when other people were present. But when they were alone she would wear her armour and not let herself be weakened by that enormous physical attraction he had for her. If she knew it for what it was and admitted it to herself, then she would not be so vulnerable, surely?

Damian and the other two were already sitting around with their drinks when Kate reached the top of the stairs, and she paused, looking down. Seen from above the large open-plan room was a picture. On the far side, to one end of the raised area in front of the wide windows, the dining table was set with écru lace mats and gleaming silver and glass. It was nowhere near dark yet, but tall white candles were alight, to either side of a bowl of pale pink rosebuds in the centre of the table.

Damian saw Kate and came up the stairs towards her. 'Come and join the party, sweetheart.' He put his arm around her and drew her close as they came down together, and she smiled up at him brilliantly. 'You look very lovely,' he whispered, loud enough for the other two to hear.

'You're looking very eye-catching yourself,' she laughed, and indeed he was, in a maroon velvet jacket and finely pleated white shirt, which threw the dark skin of his face into dramatic relief. 'What a handsome pair we make!'

She saw the faint flicker in his dark eyes, that might have been surprise, or satisfaction, or something not quite either, before he bent down and kissed her. Then Hugo was beside him, offering her a drink and brimming over with pleasure and good wishes, and Marian, looking flushed and pretty in a powder-blue crêpe dress, was adding her own once again. The celebration party had begun.

As the evening progressed it proved to be less of an ordeal than Kate had expected. Damian had evidently decided that something more than the rather casual behaviour he had shown over tea was expected of him, and he set out to play the host, as well as the newly-engaged man, as expertly as he knew how, which—with Damian—was very expertly indeed. He drew the cork from the champagne, filled their glasses, toasted his bride-to-be with just the right blend of seriousness and ardour. He attended to her wants with unobtrusive good manners. He guided the conversation, steering it away from personalities and towards stories of old Cornwall, some of which even Hugo hadn't heard before, and all of which Kate found utterly fascinating. By the time the asparagus had been followed by the duckling with its special orange sauce, and that in turn by a delicious iced confection tasting of almonds and butterscotch, the sun was setting, bathing the table and the whole room in a dull orange glow, and Kate had to admit to herself that she had never enjoyed a meal as much. When it was over and Ida had removed the remains of the feast, and they sat with their coffee watching the sky change from orange to streaky greys and greens, it seemed the most natural thing in the world for Damian to put his arm around her and pull her closer on the deep, soft settee, and for her to allow her head to rest comfortably against his maroon velvet jacket.

Through half-closed eyes she saw that Hugo had slumped back in his chair and closed his eyes wearily. Working at a quarry, even in a manager's job, would hardly be anyone's idea of light employment and it was no wonder he looked tired. She noticed the somewhat shabby dinner jacket he was wearing—such a contrast with Damian's fashionable attire—and thought it pointed up rather cruelly the gap between the two men. Damian, who had succeeded, and poor old Hugo, who had failed and was relying on the rich man's patronage. For however much Marian might eulogise about Damian's 'kindness' the fact remained that he had gained a valuable servant in Hugo, and an excellent house-keeper in Marian herself—and he knew it. There wasn't any sentiment in business, she well knew, and she wondered just how much 'kindness' he would have shown if he hadn't been able to make use of both of them.

The conversation had petered out completely and nobody seemed to want to revive it. Damian had put the record player on and the music of Gershwin filled the air plain-tively. Marian hummed softly, looking out across the green stretch of moorland with dreaming eyes. Kate allowed the music, together with the warm feeling that she had dined well and drunk a little too much champagne, to drift over her. She must have been almost asleep, for when she opened her eyes the sun had sunk into a bank of clouds and the mist was beginning to gather in the hollows of the rolling moorland.

Marian stood up, stifling a yawn, and held out her hands to Hugo. 'Come along, my lad, up you get. Remember you promised to run Ida back to the village, and it'll be dark soon.'

Hugo groaned in protest but good-humouredly allowed himself to be pulled out of the depths of his chair. He allowed his glance to rest for a moment on the two sitting so close on the settee, then remarked to nobody in particu-lar, 'Tactful wife I've got!'

Marian linked her arm with his and wrinkled her nose at him. 'Well, have you forgotten what it's like to get engaged, because I haven't. Goodnight, you two,' she added softly, 'no, don't move, you look so comfortable there.' She smiled, picked up the coffee tray, and she and Hugo went out of the room, closing the door carefully behind them.

Kate, wide awake now, was suddenly very conscious of the hard warmth of the arm that was holding her. As soon as the door was closed she drew out of the circle of Damian's grasp and moved along the settee.

'Must you?' he protested lazily. 'I was just getting used to the idea of being an engaged man. It's rather pleasant, I must admit.'

She disengaged the folds of her skirt from beneath his leg and sat up straight. 'You're exceeding the terms of the contract—isn't that how you business men would put it? Our engagement is for public consumption only, not for private amusement.' Safer to keep it light! Especially in this dusky, dreamy atmosphere!

He gave a deep chuckle. 'You seem to know the jargon.

But surely we might get a little fun out of the situation in private, too? In a mild and innocuous way, of *course*.' He slanted his devilish look at her.

'No,' said Kate, quite definitely.

'You wouldn't trust me not to overstep the contract? Or yourself?'

She stood up, walked over to a ruby-shaded lamp and, after a little fumbling with the switch, managed to turn on the light. 'I think this conversation has gone far enough. We both know that there's nothing between us but—but necessity and convenience, and I've no intention of playing at being in love. It's stupid and it's dangerous.'

'Ah!' he mocked softly. 'Then you do admit the danger?'

'I'd be a fool if I didn't,' said Kate hardily. 'You're an attractive man and I expect you could get any girl you wanted fairly easily. But you're not going to get me for a toy, Mr St Ewan. I have my own ideas about life and my own plans for living it, and you're not included in them anywhere.'

He regarded her thoughtfully and then nodded, not in the least put out. 'Well, that's straight from the shoulder and you're probably right.'

'I'm glad you agree.' She felt slightly damped by his easy, almost careless assent.

He stood up. 'Another drink?' He ignored her refusal and filled her glass again. Then he poured himself a brandy and came back and stood beside her. 'Come on, sit down and tell me something about yourself, Kate. Our public appearances are going to be fairly unconvincing if I don't know anything about the girl I'm going to marry.'

'You're not going to marry me,' she said, 'and anyway you should have considered that first, before you asked me,' she added somewhat illogically.

'I'm considering it now. And I warn you I'm not easily put off, so you may as well be comfortable.' He sat down again on the settee and patted the place beside him. She hesitated a moment and then took the chair Marian had vacated.

He shrugged, sipped his drink, and said, 'Tell me why you're so prejudiced against big business and rich men? I imagine you must be in a minority of one among girls. Certainly among the girls I've known. Don't you like the things money can buy and make possible?'

'Of course I do—in a way. I like nice clothes, pleasant surroundings. But not if it all gets too much and—and life revolves round making more and more money.' She glanced round the spacious, luxuriously-furnished room. 'I just think the simple things of life are more worth having, and where big business is concerned the simple things get crowded out. Do I sound like a horrid prig?'

He said quietly, 'You sound as if something or someone had hurt you, Kate.' He waited for a time, and when she didn't respond he said, 'Tell me about your home—your parents—relatives?'

'My parents are both dead,' she said shortly. 'My home is the flat you saw in Highgate, and I haven't any relatives.'

'What about your Miss Bebb—the one who is having the cottage? Didn't you say she was a relative?'

She shook her head. 'Nanny's a very old friend. I've always called her Nanny,' she added hastily.

There was another silence and she felt, rather than saw, his eyes resting on her thoughtfully. 'H'm,' he mused. 'Little Miss Nobody from Nowhere! You're sticking to that story?'

She moved impatiently. 'You don't really need to know about me. Why should you? You can make up some background for me, to tell people, if you really want to. I'm sure you could do it very convincingly.'

His face hardened. 'And what is that supposed to mean?'

She made herself meet his eyes. 'Just that I'm sure you're the kind of man who's never at a loss when there's something you happen to want.'

She saw the anger flash momentarily and then it was gone again. 'You don't like me very much, do you, Kate?'

'I don't know you,' she said.

'But you judge me on some flimsy idea that's floating around in your head that all rich men are scheming, calculating, dishonest, heartless monsters.'

'I wouldn't presume to judge you, Mr St Ewan,' she said distantly.

Before she knew what he intended to do he had leaned forward, gripped her wrist and pulled her out of her chair, to land, not very gracefully, on the settee beside him again. Eyes wide, she tried to pull her hand away, but it was held in a steely grip.

'Let me go!' she hissed, struggling ineffectually.

'Not on your life.' His voice was grim. 'Not until we've got things straightened out, and I can't talk to you when you're sitting halfway across the room.'

'About three feet away——' she disputed.

'Shut up and listen.' He shook her arm not very gently. 'Now look, Kate, I'm trying hard to keep my temper, but you're not making it very easy for me. I can see you've got some stupid and illogical prejudice against me or against my kind. I don't know why, and you apparently don't intend me to know. Well, fair enough, you don't have to tell me if you don't want to. But you've made a contract with me—a business contract, if you'll forgive me putting it like that—and I intend to see that you carry out your side of it.'

'I thought I did rather well tonight, when Marian and Hugo were here,' she said in a small voice, because her wrist was hurting where his fingers pressed into it.

'Oh, you did. You put on an excellent show. It even convinced me.'

She stared up at him, horrified. 'You mean you thought I—I'd fallen for you?'

He smiled thinly. 'Let's say I thought you might be enjoying the situation.'

'Well, I wasn't, I assure you. I was just acting for all I was worth.'

'All right, so I was wrong. But what I'm saying to you is that you can't gaze swooningly at me when other people are present, and then fight like a tiger cat when we're alone. My nervous system won't stand it,' he added with that devilish look she was beginning to recognise.

'I don't fight you,' she said. 'You started it.' She tried again to pull away from him.

He still held her tightly. 'There are more ways than one of fighting,' he said, 'and a woman's way is often the most deadly, or hasn't anyone told you that? Suppose we call a truce, Kate? I may have been ill-advised to start this thing, I think now that probably I have. But we can't either of us back out now because we depend on each other, so can't we be civilised about it? If we have to put on a loving act in public, at least let's be business colleagues when we're on our own—working together towards the same goal, trusting each other.'

'Is that what business colleagues do?' she asked in a small, bitter voice, thinking of her father's business colleague, his closest and most trusted friend, who had quite ruthlessly, to serve his own ends, caused her father's bankruptcy and almost certainly his death. 'Do they trust each other?'

'That's the way I work,' he said simply.

'And would you trust me like that? When you hardly know me?'

'Yes, I would,' he said without emotion, releasing her wrist. 'If you can judge me, then surely I can do the same to you.'

She looked at him uncertainly. Was he being sincere or was this just smooth talk? And—even more important—had she convinced him that she had merely been play-acting when she had nestled so softly against him while the music was playing and the light was fading? The very thought that he might have guessed what a devastating effect his nearness had on her made her want to curl up and sink into the ground, out of sight of those searching dark eyes. Somehow she must manage to be more careful in future.

'Well,' he urged, 'what do you say? Friends and partners, Kate, and no emotional overtones—except in public, of course?'

'Yes,' she said. There seemed nothing else to say.

'Good,' he said briskly. 'Let's shake hands on that.' His handclasp was firm and brief. 'Now then, we'd better make some plans. You'll need to buy clothes, so I suggest you let Marian take you into town tomorrow morning. She has friends in the trade, as she told you, and she'll be useful to you. I'll let you have a blank cheque. You'll have to forgo your dislike of filthy lucre on this occasion,' he added with a grin. 'However much you hate it, you must remember that the Lindsays will believe you're my promised bride, so do yourself proud. Which reminds me of something . . .' He stood up. 'Wait for me a moment,' he said, and went swiftly across the room and up the stairs.

Before Kate had time to feel surprise he was back, carrying a small leather box. He sat on the arm of the settee and opened it to disclose an exquisite string of milky-white pearls.

'I'd like you to wear these on appropriate occasions. Let's see how they look on you.' He leaned over and clasped the pearls round her neck so swiftly that she scarcely felt the touch of his fingers on her skin. Then he stood up and moved away a little. 'Yes, very nice. You have a beautiful neck, Kate.' He sounded as if he were admiring a sculpture. 'Pearls suit you.'

She did what any woman would do—she looked round for a mirror, but there wasn't one in the room. 'They're real?' she asked, very much at a loss. Silly question, of course they were. The St Ewans wouldn't go in for department store pearls.

'Oh yes, they're real—not even cultured, I believe. They were my mother's,' he added without any particular emotion. 'The rest of her jewellery is at the bank, but I always keep these at home. Pearls are sensitive creatures—you can't just stack them away in a vault and forget about them or they lose their value.' He stood back, eyes narrowed, assessing the effect. 'Yes, very attractive. It completes the effect. You'll wear them?' It sounded more like a command than a request.

He evidently didn't see any reason why he shouldn't make use of his mother's pearls to further his own plans. It was a pity he wasn't as sensitive as the pearls were. 'Oh yes, of course I'll wear them, if you want me to,' she said coolly. 'I'd like you to keep them, though, until I need them. I shouldn't care to take the responsibility.'

'As you wish,' he said carelessly. 'Keep them on now and take a look at yourself when you go upstairs. I'll have them back in the morning. And now, if you'll excuse me, I have some letters to write. I'll leave the cheque with Marian in case I don't see you at breakfast. Hugo and I have to leave early for a meeting with the workers' council. I'll be home for lunch and in the afternoon I'd like you to come with me on a short tour of the St Ewan domain, so that I can put you in the picture. Will that suit you?' he inquired politely.

'Of course,' she said in the same tone. 'I'm sure it will be very interesting.'

He glanced quickly at her, seemed to be about to say something, and then stopped. Finally he said formally, 'That's all settled, then. Thank you for being so co-operative. Goodnight, Kate.'

He stood looking at her for a moment, the dark eyes inscrutable. Then, with a small, courteous bow, and not coming an inch closer to her, he went swiftly across the room and up the stairs. She watched him as he reached the top and walked along the gallery to a door at the end, furthest from her own room. It would have been natural and friendly to look down at her and smile, but he went in and closed the door without a backward glance.

She turned away and fumbled with the clasp of the pearls, but couldn't manage to undo it. As the pearls were very valuable the clasp would be of a safety variety and tricky to open unless you were familiar with it. For some reason she couldn't wait to get the pearls off and she hurried upstairs to her room and sat down before the mirror to wrestle with the intricacies of the beautiful diamond clasp. With the mirror reflection to help her she solved the problem easily and she took off the pearls cautiously and sat looking down at them, lying in her hand. Pearls suit you, he had said. And, you have a beautiful neck, Kate. Slowly she lifted them again and held them round her neck without fastening the clasp. The silky smoothness was like a caress against her skin.

Then she heard a door open at the end of the gallery and the sound of a man's footsteps approaching, muffled by the carpet, but still audible. She sat stiffly, staring at her reflection in the mirror, every nerve taut. The footsteps came nearer, paused for a moment outside her door, then went on again.

Her shoulders slumped and she felt energy draining out of her, with an odd, empty feeling inside that might have been relief. Or disappointment.

Very slowly she arranged the pearls in their velvet-lined box, snapped down the lid, and began to get ready for bed.

Kate had not expected ever again to buy clothes without so much as a glance at the price tag. But as she and Marian loaded the result of her shopping expedition into the back of Marian's small car next morning she felt slightly dizzy at the thought of the amount of Damian's money she had spent. She hoped he would consider the result worth the cost.

Marian came out of the small, elegant boutique owned by her friend Louise, carrying the last of the large, flat boxes, and stacked it on top of the rest. 'That's the lot,' she declared happily. 'Now there's just shoes, and then it'll be time to go along to the Grand and meet Damian.'

Damian and Hugo had left before Kate got down for breakfast, but before he went he had left a cheque for her with Marian. 'He said this was in case you hadn't any credit arrangements with your own bank,' Marian explained. Kate almost laughed aloud at this fresh demonstration of his unbelievable attention to detail, when he had something planned out. Naturally, he wouldn't want Marian to think that his fiancée couldn't afford to buy her own clothes.

'And we're meeting him at the Grand for a drink at mid-day,' Marian had gone on to explain. 'Then I'm going to drive back here to welcome the Graysons and get them installed and familiar with the working of the house, and Damian will give you lunch and take you over to see the quarry. All right?'

'All right,' Kate had said, and found it not too difficult to smile in happy anticipation. To her surprise she found herself looking forward to seeing the main source of the St Ewan family fortune, but she couldn't have said why.

Now, leaving Marian's car outside the boutique, in a side street, they walked back to the town shopping centre. Marian was delighted with their purchases. 'What did you think of Louise, Kate? She's rather a pet, isn't she, but very keen too. She and I were apprentices together, and she was always really dedicated to clothes and fashion, and she's awfully clever at it. She had a whale of a time fitting you out, I could see. You're every saleswoman's dream, Kate, you've got such a gorgeous figure. It's a pity it's the end of the season, but you'll be able to buy lots of lovely autumn and winter things when she gets the new stock in.'

'Yes,' said Kate brightly, wondering where she would be by the time autumn came. Her wonderful plan to move into the cottage with Nanny and get some sort of job didn't seem quite so wonderful any more. She didn't know why she was having doubts about the idea; it was something to do with a need she was beginning to feel to remove herself entirely from Damian St Ewan's vicinity once this charade of the engagement was over.

Marian was chatting on about the clothes they had bought: stunningly colourful beach wear, cashmere sweaters for cool days, silky little dresses that would squeeze to nothing in your hand but fall into beautiful lines on your body, longer dresses for more formal occasions. There was a fabulous printed poncho from Italy, red and white splashed on dull black rayon. And the evening dresses were dreams—all English, for Louise said that English designers were tops when it came to evening dresses . . . Kate sighed, listening to Marian's raptures. She couldn't deny that she had loved every exciting moment she had spent in Louise's elegant boutique. But now that it was over and the results were lying in flat lilac-coloured boxes in the back of Marian's car, it all seemed futile and pointless. For a time she had almost believed herself to be a happy girl, about to be married to a man she loved. Crazy thought! As if she could ever love a man like Damian St Ewan! And as if he would give the little typist he had persuaded to play a small part in his intricate plans another thought when those plans were finalised!

They were entering a shoe shop now. 'Let's get this over as quickly as we can,' Kate said with sudden impatience, and then, seeing the look of disappointment on Marian's face, she added. 'I can't wait to get to the Grand.' Marian would understand *that* sort of impatience.

The Grand was a large, opulent-looking hotel overlooking the bay, with palm trees fringing smooth green lawns in front, and expensive cars pulled up at the side. Kate was glad she had decided to wear one of the new dresses she had just bought—a perky little number in lime green. She caught a glimpse of herself in a long mirror as they went into the hotel and hardly recognised the girl that looked back at her. Louise had been right, that shade of green was just right with her shiny, near-black hair, and all that exciting trying-on of dresses had given her cheeks a glow that hadn't been there before. Damian ought to be satisfied, she thought wryly, she looked very like a blissfully happy, newly-engaged girl.

'We're meeting in the Fisherman's Bar,' Marian said. 'It's cosier than the big lounge. Damian always goes there.'

'You go first, you know the way.' Kate followed Marian across the foyer, crowded with visitors on their way in to lunch. Any minute now she would see Damian again, and the prospect gave her a sinking feeling inside. This would be their first appearance together in public. They would probably meet people he knew; she hoped she wouldn't let him down.

Then they passed through a doorway and she saw him. He was sitting on a high stool at the far end of a curved bar, and behind him, as part of the décor, fishing nets were draped over the wall. He might almost have been a Cornish fisherman himself, in blue canvas trousers and a shirt of some roughish oatmeal material. He had a look of the sea and the open air, with his dark hair appreciably longer and more undisciplined than when Kate had first seen him, before he went to Canada. It was difficult to remember, now, that polished city executive he had been then. His expression, too, seemed to have altered and lost its tension. He looked younger, tougher, infinitely more—what was the word?—more abrasive.

He saw them and got to his feet. His eyes met Kate's across the long room, filled with chatter and smoke and the clink of glasses, and she stopped, not knowing that she had done so. For a moment out of time they stared at each other and the room seemed to swing round crazily. Then Kate gave herself a little shake and followed Marian.

Damian was coming towards them now, smiling. 'You're prompt,' he said, putting an arm behind each girl and propelling them towards the bar. He pulled out stools for them. 'Two young women shopping for clothes and you're actually only three minutes behind time, it's quite unbelievable. What will you drink, both of you?'

Marian, as she was driving, plumped for tomato juice, and Kate said she would have the same. When the tall, frosty glass was placed in front of her she looked at it with surprise. Everything suddenly had a new colour and sparkle to it, and life had become curiously unreal. She sat on the high stool and sipped her iced drink, tangy with Worcester sauce, and only part of her seemed to be there at all. She heard the other two talking and she supposed she joined in intelligibly, but she couldn't be sure of that, either. She was aware that Damian was being greeted by newcomers as they entered the bar; indeed, he seemed to know and be known by everyone here. She felt that eyes were upon her, as a stranger and Damian's companion, but nothing signified. She felt so strangely light-headed that she began to wonder if she were going to be ill.

Then, as quickly as it had come, the feeling passed and the room swung back to normal again. Marian was saying, 'No, thanks, I won't stay for another drink. I must hurry back to be in time to receive my excellent Graysons. Some friends are giving them a lift from Exeter,' she added to Kate, 'and they may be earlier than they said. I'll drive very carefully with all your precious loot in the back, Kate.' She drained her glass, and, waving away Damian's offer to see her to her car, hurried away.

Marian's departure seemed to be the signal for them to be joined by various men who appeared to be Damian's acquaintances or business associates. The news of the engagement was evidently getting around already, and Kate, flushed and pretty, and feeling as tipsy as if she had been drinking something much more potent than tomato juice, found herself in the centre of a flatteringly interested company, being introduced and complimented. Damian's arm was firm around her and she laughed up into his eyes, as sparklingly happy as any engaged girl might be expected to be. When the last of the men had drifted off to lunch he murmured, close to her ear, 'Well done, little one, that was entirely convincing.' Then his expression changed. 'Oh, lord,' he groaned, 'now we're in for it!'

A heavily built man was approaching them, a hand raised in greeting. Kate recognised him as the man they had encountered briefly in the harbour car park yesterday morning, when they were leaving the train. It was Carole Oliver's father.

'Ha! Damian! Well met, indeed!' His tone was expansive, somewhat over-jovial. He looked expectantly towards Kate.

'Hullo, John.' Damian sounded civil but not particularly enthusiastic. 'Kate, this is John Oliver, a business colleague of mine. John, Kate Warrington, my fiancée.'

John Oliver was probably in his forties, but looked older.

He was florid, with moist blue eyes, and was several stone over weight. He sandwiched Kate's hand between two large, podgy ones. 'My word, but you've found yourself a beauty, old son. I thought . . .' He stopped, looking suddenly uncomfortable, and Kate wondered just how unflatteringly Carole had described her to her family. She could imagine.

'A real beauty,' repeated Carole's father rather lamely.

Damian smiled and put an arm round Kate's waist. 'Thanks for pointing it out, John,' he said drily. 'I might not have noticed it myself.'

John Oliver roared with laughter and thumped him playfully on the shoulder. 'Ha! Very good, very good! Does he make jokes at your expense, my dear? You've got to watch your young man. Myself, I never quite know when he's being serious and when he isn't. Now, what are you both drinking?'

To Kate's relief Damian thanked him but refused firmly. 'We've got a luncheon engagement. We must be on our way. You ready, darling?'

Mr Oliver's face fell. 'Ah, and I was hoping you'd let me buy you lunch here. But never mind, you must come along for drinks this evening instead. My wife's looking forward to meeting the little lady.' He beamed at Kate. 'Usual time, Damian. I expect you'll find a bit of a mob there, but you're used to that, aren't you?'

Damian thanked him, urging Kate towards the door of the bar at the same time. The last thing she saw of Mr Oliver was a large hand waving to them round the corner of what purported to be the mast of a fishing boat.

Outside the hotel they got into Damian's car, a beautiful, low-slung monster. 'Phew, that was a close shave!' He eased the car out on to the promenade. 'I wouldn't want to have to put our engagement to the test of a lunch with John Oliver—not yet. You might not think it, but he's as keen as they're made and a great one for sniffing out discrepancies.'

'And you consider me a discrepancy?' Kate inquired, somewhat dashed.

107

He removed a hand from the wheel and patted her arm. 'You did very well, my child,' he said. 'And you looked quite delightful—all my friends were eaten with jealousy. But I wouldn't be unfair enough to expose you to John Oliver's probing curiosity just yet—not until you know enough about me and my affairs to make our engagement entirely plausible. I thought we might spend an hour or two on a conducted tour.'

'But you said we had a luncheon engagement?'

'So we have,' he smiled. 'How would it appeal to you to buy in some food and have a picnic? Or would you rather have a pukka hotel meal?'

'Oh, no,' said Kate quickly, 'I love picnics, and it's much too hot to eat indoors when we can eat outside. Shall I go and shop for food?'

She found a supermarket with a delicatessen, and returned to the car some time later with bulging carrier bags. 'I've been very clever and even remembered to buy knives and spoons from Woolworths,' she announced smugly. 'Two of each and some disposable picnic plates. How's that for efficiency?' She felt suddenly extraordinarily gay and light-hearted.

He helped her to load in the bags. 'And I, madam, have been equally efficient. I've bought in a bottle of wine and borrowed a couple of glasses from my wine merchant. We'll have ourselves a feast. Now, let's go!'

The engine sprang into purring life and within minutes they were out of the town and heading south for the coast. 'I know a good place to picnic,' Damian said. 'The beaches will be crowded, so we'll keep away from them.' He turned the car off the main road presently and into a maze of lanes so narrow that two cars couldn't have passed each other. Fortunately they didn't meet another car.

'It's like threading old rope through the eye of a small needle,' Kate said, and he laughed and replied, 'Don't you dare compare my car with old rope!' and it was all very easy and friendly.

They parked the car high on a grassy cliff overlooking a

sandy cove, where far below sunbathers lay stretched out on the sands and children played and shouted and ran in and out of the edge of the waves.

Kate munched a sausage roll, spooned out a creamy salad concoction from a plastic beaker and sighed contentedly. 'And to think I might now be fighting my way along Oxford Street to the Wimpey Bar!'

Damian, leaning on one elbow, smiled his devilish smile. 'Has it been worth all the trauma, then?'

She pretended to consider that. 'I'll let you know later, when the performance is over.'

He tossed down the remains of a glass of wine and stretched out on the grass, hands behind his head, eyes closed. Kate sat and looked at the long length of him lying beside her. How brown the skin of his arms was, and his neck where his shirt fell open. She could see the old-fashioned gold locket quite clearly now; it had a thin cover, hiding the picture behind. The breeze ruffled his hair and blew a thick strand across his forehead. The oatmeal shirt was a bloused style and, as he lay straight on the grass, it had parted from his trousers at the waist to show a bare midriff, as brown as his face. 'Do you swim a lot?' she asked suddenly, and he opened his eyes and looked up at her under long curving lashes.

'I do,' he said, and added in a lazy amused voice, 'I'm much the same colour all over. I'll give you a demonstration some day.' The grin widened and he added, 'A swimming demonstration, of course.'

She felt the colour rise hotly into her face and began to gather together the remains of their lunch, sitting back on her heels and half turned away from him. 'Do you want any more to eat?' she said, 'because if not shouldn't we be going?'

He make no attempt to move. 'I'm not sure that I want to go, it's so pleasant here. Suppose we stayed for a while?' he mused. 'Now, how could we pass the time, do you think?'

'I don't know,' said Kate shortly, struggling to push the

cork back into the half-empty bottle of wine. She wouldn't turn and look at him—she *wouldn't* because if she did——

She went on fumbling with the cork, her whole body warm with a treacherous awareness of the man lying beside her. She knew she had only to turn, to move a hand towards him and she would be pulled down into his arms, held close against him, his mouth on hers—— Her hand trembled, the cork slipped and the remainder of the wine poured out on to the grass with a gurgle.

'Damn!' she exploded angrily.

Damian pulled himself into a sitting position. 'Never mind,' he told her mildly. 'The sun's been on it too long, and I never did care much for boiled Liebfraumilch.' He pulled a blade of grass and sat chewing it, regarding her with a quizzical expression. 'Poor Kate, it's a shame to tease you, but you look so pretty when you blush. Don't worry, I wasn't going to suggest anything improper. We made a contract, and when I make a contract I stick to it. I'm a business man, remember? The kind of man you hate most.'

She refused to rise to the bait, said nothing, and went on tidying up.

'What's your dream man like, Kate?' he inquired lazily. 'You must have a type in mind? Most girls dream of marrying for money, but not you, of course. What *would* you marry for?'

'Love,' she said.

'Oh, naturally,' he mocked. 'I never doubted that. But what profession would qualify?'

'I don't know,' she said impatiently. She stood up and shook out her skirt. 'A farmer, perhaps.'

He laughed. 'Farmers are just as much money-motivated as anyone else these days, didn't you know?'

'Well, then, a doctor—or a vet—or something like that.' She picked up one of the bags. 'Is the inquisition over?'

He got to his feet, smiling. 'For the moment. We'll now go on a quick tour and you shall see how and where the horrid tycoon makes all his millions. Come along.'

She followed him to the car and climbed in with what

she hoped was a modicum of dignity and an uncomfortable feeling that she was engaged in some sort of game in which the odds were so stacked against her that she was bound to lose.

CHAPTER SEVEN

KATE was beginning to find out that Damian St Ewan had two characteristic paces for action. One was slow, easy, lazily relaxed. The other—and this was where his business activities were concerned—was as intense as a high-voltage cable. What he called his 'quick tour' was indeed quick, and she began to feel quite dizzy as she was whisked from scene to scene in rapid succession.

They called first at his impressive office suite in Truro, with a battery of brass plates with company names at the entrance.

'Do you own all these?' she inquired, 'all these different companies?' She was trying not to feel a certain admiration for any man who could keep as many balls in the air all at once.

He smiled and admitted that he had a controlling interest in all of them. 'But you're not interested in the business side, are you?' he added with a touch of irony, 'so when I've checked with my secretary that nothing urgent has cropped up since this morning we'll go down to the coast and see how the boat-building is progressing.'

At the boatyard in the small fishing village on the south coast Kate saw two large fishing boats in construction for a new co-operative venture that Damian, it seemed, was financing. Kate was fascinated by the work that was going on here. The workmen were craftsmen, of a type as sturdily independent as all craftsmen. But from the head man down to the young apprentice they treated Damian with the easy familiarity of a fellow worker. 'They like him,' Kate thought.

'Even if he is the man with the money, they don't resent him.' She was very quiet as they went back to the car, and listened in silence as Damian told her how he hoped, later on, to establish a new processing plant, canning or freezing, whichever seemed most appropriate when the time came.

'But that's only in the drawing-board stage as yet. The main thing is to get the fishing going again. You know, Kate,' he mused, as the big car turned north again, eating up the smooth main roads, 'Cornwall's much more than a pretty face turned to the tourist trade—although that has its part to play. But you don't have to go very far from the cream teas and the plastic piskies to find the old tough Cornwall, and that's what we're trying to help to preserve —some of us.'

From her corner in the front seat of the car she cast a glance up at his profile and saw the firm set of the mouth, the jut of the chin. She tried to tell herself that this was just the way he explained to himself the urge to speculate, to make more money. The way he justified being a very rich man. But she was finding it increasingly difficult to think of him as only a hard, ruthless man of business. There was more than one side to Damian St Ewan.

'The quarry next,' he said. 'You shall see the chief source of the disgusting St Ewan wealth.'

'You don't let me forget my prejudice, do you?' said Kate, with a wry smile. She wanted him to follow that up, to ask her if she was changing her opinion of him. In a vague sort of way she wanted to put their relationship on a different, perhaps a deeper, level. But he concentrated on his driving and made no reply.

At the quarry Hugo was very much in charge. While he and Damian talked business in one of the low office buildings Kate stared down, overwhelmed, at the great crater in the earth that stretched below her. Right down at the bottom, looking like ants, men were working with trucks, or perched up in cranes that waved slowly above the grey depths. Far away on the other side of the crater a line of trucks was moving up a steep gradient, powered by some invisible source. At the top of the rise there were lorries, lifting gear, great piles of slate.

Hugo came and stood beside her at the window. 'Well, what do you think of our little set-up?' She heard the pride in his voice.

'Little! It's sensational. It reminds me of pictures of a lunar landscape. It makes you feel as if it's been here since the beginning of time.'

Hugo looked pleased and he would have taken her on a tour of the whole quarry if Damian hadn't intervened. 'Another day, Hugo, we must get back now. We're going to the Olivers for drinks and Kate will want time to pretty up, won't you, darling? Not that she needs to,' he added, and he leaned down and kissed the tip of her nose.

As they drove away down the rough dusty road, a gang of workmen recognised Damian's car and waved cheerily. He waved back and shouted a greeting. 'They're a grand bunch of fellows,' he told Kate. 'My father treated them well and he never had any labour troubles, and they've transferred their loyalty to me—which is lucky for me.' The big car turned out on to the main road again. 'Well, that's all there is to see just now. Do you think you're familiar enough with my interests to keep your end up at the Olivers?'

'Yes, I think so,' Kate said slowly. 'But aren't I going to see the mine? I thought it was the chief reason for my being here.'

He glanced quickly at her and then back at the road. 'There's nothing to see at Wheal Dora,' he said. 'You wouldn't be interested.'

She was surprised at the sudden stab of disappointment she felt. It was as if he had closed a door in her face. She sensed that Wheal Dora meant very much more to him than just a few old buildings, but he had refused to talk to her about the place, refused to take her there. Oh well, why should he share his plans and ambitions with her? And why should she feel so hurt because he would not?

Nevertheless, the friendly atmosphere that had been growing between them at the boatyard and at the quarry seemed to be spoilt and for the rest of the drive back to Trestenak Damian was quiet and withdrawn. As for Kate, a totally uncharacteristic feeling of irritation seemed to have taken possession of her, which persisted through her preparations for the evening ahead, and was still there as they stood together in the Olivers' elegant drawing room, some hours later, sipping the Olivers' drinks and playing the social game with the Olivers' well-heeled friends.

Kate hadn't expected to enjoy their visit to the Oliver residence and she certainly wasn't enjoying it. From the moment she walked into the room beside Damian she had felt a strain. It was nothing that she could put her finger on, for John Oliver was almost embarrassingly hospitable and attentive to her, and his wife, elegantly dressed and coif- fured and perfumed, seemed to be going out of her way to be charming.

'Damian's given us all such a *lovely* surprise,' she cried, holding both Kate's hands. 'It'll be such *fun* having parties and things all together.' She wrinkled her nose at Damian and said archly, 'Bachelors are such a bore, and it's been so wicked of you living all alone in that great-big house.' The carefully-shaped mouth smiled brightly, hostess-fashion, but the blue eyes were busy summing up Kate's hair-style, her face, her dress. It was of crisp white cotton, Swiss- embroidered, with a full flounced skirt. Louise had been in raptures about it. 'Marvellous with Kate's dark hair and her lovely skin with that tinge of pink,' she had sighed. 'So romantic!' Kate tried to encourage herself now by re- membering those words as she suffered Mrs Oliver's scrutiny and knew she was wondering what it was that Kate had and Carole hadn't. But if she was disappointed on her daughter's account she wasn't going to show it.

'Damian, take Kate around, do,' she cooed. 'Everyone's just longing to meet her.' She moved away, the lurex trim- ming on her lilac crêpe glistening.

At that moment Carole herself appeared in the doorway,

a young man on each side of her. She wore a startling flame-coloured outfit that displayed rather than covered her lovely curves and she was flirting vivaciously with the young men, who were in their early twenties and had pleasant boyish faces which they had endeavoured to conceal with odd tufts of hair in various places around their chins and cheeks.

Carole had evidently forgotten her rage of yesterday, or had decided to conceal it. Seeing Damian and Kate, she waved and cried gaily, 'Hullo, you two!' She took a hand of each of her escorts and pulled them across the room. 'Come along, dearies, you simply *must* see Damian's latest.'

Damian's latest! Just as if I were a new exhibit in a zoo, thought Kate, and seethed inwardly.

'Bernie, Tom, meet Miss—er——'

'Warrington,' supplied Kate, at the same moment that Damian said, 'Kate,' and the two boys laughed and shook hands and looked faintly embarrassed.

Carole put a languid hand on Damian's sleeve and gazed up at him with her own special brand of insolent intimacy. 'Poor old love,' she crooned. 'It had to happen some day, you can't play the field for ever and not get caught, can you?'

Kate watched Damian's face. She knew that he was quite capable of annihilating the girl with a couple of well-chosen words or an icy glance, if he so cared. But he evidently didn't care; his expression was as tolerant as that of an adoring uncle of a horror infant.

Carole let her eyes slide over Kate from head to foot. 'What a pretty dress,' she drawled. 'How clever of you to be able to wear white, I do envy you. I always think white has a sort of extinguishing effect, if you know what I mean. Unless you're the right type for it, of course.'

'Of course,' agreed Kate coolly. And I'm the right type, she added to herself, fuming. Dead easy to extinguish. Telling retorts began to suggest themselves, but she pushed them away. It was no part of her brief to be rude to

Damian's friends, however rude he was prepared to allow them to be to her.

As Carole drifted away again, laughing up provocatively at her two escorts, he observed in a low, amused, and—yes —affectionate voice, 'Carole loves to do her sex-kitten act! You can see why she wouldn't have made a convincing fiancée, as you suggested. She's just a kid, as yet.'

Kate lifted a dark eyebrow and said sweetly, 'No doubt she'll fill the bill very well later on.'

She saw the small frown that flickered over his face, but he made no retort. He put a hand at her elbow. 'Come on,' he said, his lips compressed, 'let's mingle.'

They mingled. Conversation rose in volume as the drinks circulated. There must have been twenty or more people in the room and everybody seemed to know everybody else and the talk was about events and people of which Kate knew nothing. They were friendly enough, they tried to include her, but gradually her head began to ache and the smile seemed to be frozen on her lips. She glanced at Damian, so much at ease, and she thought that these were his people; they were not hers and never would be, and it seemed suddenly unkind of him to have brought her here. Unkind and unnecessary. It was the Lindsays from Canada that she had been hired to impress, and the Lindsays wouldn't be here until the day after tomorrow. Somebody thrust another drink into her hand and after a moment or two she put the glass down on a side table. She wondered how much longer Damian would want to stay.

Then Carole came up and linked her arm through his. 'Damian darling, Daddy wants a word with you in the morning room—something about some committee or other —he asked me to find you.'

He looked round for Kate, frowning slightly, and Carole said quickly, 'Oh, your girl-friend'll be all right, I'll get someone to amuse her.' She lifted her voice above the chatter. 'Tim, come over here, there's a love.'

A fair man with a thin, intelligent face and humorous eyes, whom Kate hadn't seen before, joined them. 'Tim, look after Damian's girl, there's a sweetie. Get her a drink or something,' she ordered carelessly. 'Come on, Damian. Daddy's waiting—he's got some man with him.'

Damian turned to Kate with a small shrug, not looking particularly pleased. 'Excuse me,' he said, and allowed himself to be led away.

The fair man smiled crookedly. 'That wasn't much of an introduction, was it? Trust Carole to be scatty about it. Name of Turner, local medico. And you're——?'

'Kate Warrington. I'm here with Damian St Ewan.'

'Ah!' Understanding dawned and with it interest. 'So you're the girl who has done the impossible and captured the hitherto invincible Mr St Ewan. I must say I approve of his taste.'

'Thank you,' said Kate.

'Would you like a drink?' He grimaced towards the crush around the bar and when Kate shook her head he looked relieved. 'Well, why don't we go out and get a breath of fresh air? I don't know about you, but I feel that my oxygen level is in poor shape.'

Kate hesitated, wondering how long Damian would be. But there was no sign of him, and she was longing for some cool air on her aching forehead. Anyway, she decided, he would find her easily enough when he returned, so she followed the doctor through the open patio window on to the terrace outside.

They leaned on the balustrade and looked out over the spacious gardens. The doctor sighed. 'Quite something, aren't they? There's a swimming pool round the side, and tennis courts there behind the trees. Why did I take up medicine instead of china clay? I hear your young man's hoping to go into the tin business. Interesting, that. These old tin mines are quite a landmark in Cornwall and the St Ewan one is a particularly good specimen, don't you think?'

'I don't know, I haven't seen it,' Kate admitted.

'Really?' He sounded surprised. 'I'd have thought Damian St Ewan would have taken you out there to show it off. He's known to be almost fanatically dedicated to the project of reopening it. It's not far from here—I think you can see the top of the stack, it stands fairly high.' He raised himself on his hands on the balustrade and peered over the top of the shrubbery surrounding the gardens. 'Yes, it's getting a bit dark, but you can just see it against the sky. See that single elm at the margin of the wall? Well, if you look a little to the right of it—let me lift you up a bit.' He put an arm round her waist, raising her a couple of inches off the ground. 'See it now?'

A light laugh sounded behind them and Kate slid out of the doctor's grasp to see Carole standing in the window, with Damian behind her, looking grimmer than she had seen him look before.

'Ah, here she is,' cried Carole gaily. 'Damian thought you'd run off with his lady love, Timmy.'

The doctor grinned. 'That's an idea too,' he remarked equably. 'Let me know if you're considering it at any time, Kate, I'd like first refusal.'

He was fooling, of course, just as the men in the Fisherman's Bar had been fooling this morning, with their extravagant compliments. This morning Damian had laughed, but he wasn't laughing now. His mouth was a hard, unsmiling line. 'Are you ready, Kate?' he said curtly, and, to Carole, 'Say goodbye to your mother for us, will you? We won't interrupt her.' His hand was at Kate's elbow. 'Come along—darling.' The 'darling' was, she realised, an afterthought.

They got into the car in silence. Damian was upset and angry about something, that was very clear, but he couldn't be angry with her. She certainly hadn't done anything he could take exception to.

She could hardly have been more wrong. As soon as the Daimler had traversed the length of the drive and reached the road he stopped the engine and turned on her furiously. 'Well, that was a pretty poor show you put on this evening. You'll have to do better than that, you know.'

She gasped. 'I don't know what you're talking about. What have I done?'

'What you've done is to make me look a fool. You've hardly troubled to conceal how bored you were all evening. And then, when I was called away on a business matter for a few minutes, you couldn't just wait for me, could you?' He laughed nastily. 'Oh no, you had to slink outside with that doctor fellow.'

Kate stared at him, hardly able to believe her own ears. 'We're alone now,' she said. 'There isn't any need for you to put on a big jealousy act.'

'Jealousy nothing,' he flung at her inelegantly. 'As far as I'm concerned you can have as many doctors as you like with their arms around you. I seem to remember that doctors figured high on your priority list of men. But at least you might have had the decency to wait until our contract is put through satisfactorily before you start casting your line. You know damn well that Carole isn't taking our engagement seriously. She doesn't know the facts, of course, but she's suspicious, and if she goes throwing hints about to the Lindsays—and she's bound to meet them while they're here—the whole thing could come unstuck.'

'Rubbish!' returned Kate with spirit. 'That's absolutely unreasonable. And anyway, if you think you have cause to complain, so have I. How can you possibly expect me to look as if I'm enjoying myself when you allow that girl to treat me as if I were some—some tart you'd brought in off the streets!' She was really angry now and she wasn't choosing her words either.

He glared at her. 'Don't be so damned touchy. Carole's not like that.'

'If I'm touchy, then so are you,' she shot back at him. And somewhere in the back of her mind came the thought, We're quarrelling—how extraordinary! 'As a matter of fact,' she went on, 'I may as well tell you that he didn't have his arms round me. He was merely lifting me up so that he could point out Wheal Dora to me.'

'So that he could——' He sounded as if he were going to explode in exasperation. 'And what the hell does Doctor Timothy Turner know about the mine anyway?' He managed to make the name sound ridiculous.

Kate said coldly, 'He seemed surprised that you hadn't shown it to me already. Everybody seems to know that it's your special interest, and I suppose they expected that I would have known all about it.'

His mouth was set into a hard, straight line. 'All right then, we'll go and see it. Now.'

'Now?' She looked through the car window into the shadow lane. 'But it's nearly dark.'

'Don't argue,' he said curtly, stretching out to switch on the engine. 'You want to see Wheal Dora and you shall see it.'

Kate sighed. And they said women were the unreasonable sex! But as Damian drove the powerful car a little too fast along the narrow lanes she was not in the least dismayed by his anger. On the contrary, and for some reason that she couldn't quite understand, she felt oddly excited and stimulated. It must be because she was going to see this mysterious Wheal Dora at last.

After about ten minutes Damian turned off the lane on to a stony track that seemed to lead into the moor and then stop. He brought the car to a halt. 'We'll have to walk from here. There used to be a proper road, but no longer, of course.'

They got out of the car and he glanced down at Kate in her white dress 'You look like a little ghost in this light,' he said. 'Haven't you got a wrap of some sort with you?'

She shook her head. 'I didn't expect to be taking a walk in the country. It's a warm evening, and anyway I'm sure ghosts don't feel the cold.'

She thought he smiled, but she couldn't be sure. 'Look where you're going,' he said. 'The ground's pretty rough.' His hand closed over her bare arm and her senses suddenly responded to his touch so that she stumbled and lurched against him.

'I *told* you to be careful.' His arm went round her, pulling her close, and thus linked they walked on across the stubbly turf. The light was fading every moment into deep, soft dusk. Behind them the sky was quite dark, but ahead the dying glow of the sunset turned the clouds to pale yellow as they merged with grey mist. They walked on in a silence that had somehow become companionable, until they reached the top of the rising ground.

Damian stopped. 'There it is,' he said. 'There's Wheal Dora.'

Kate had seen photographs of the old derelict mine buildings that are dotted about the West Cornwall landscape and this one looked to her much the same as the others. But what she heard in Damian St Ewan's voice told her that to him it was unique and special.

'This was the engine house.' As they came up to the tallish, plain building he put out a hand and touched the stone. 'We had one of the first steam engines to be used in Cornwall. That was way back in the last century. It was a very large mine in its day, but all the rest of the buildings have decayed into nothing and this is all that remains— this and the stack. They built the stacks to last for ever.' He patted the tall, tapering round chimney that reared up against the sky like a giant finger pointing.

Kate stared up at all that was left of Wheal Dora. Weeds and bushes were growing rank around the base of the stone buildings and creepers were crawling upwards, smothering the original shape and winding in and out of the empty gaping windows. And suddenly, with a catch in her throat, she felt the pathos of this place, standing here alone and deserted year after year, in the middle of no-where, crumbling away from neglect. A place that had once teemed with life and activity, with men working and machinery turning, proudly contributing to the needs of the country to which it belonged. She turned to Damian, standing a dark shadow just behind her.

'Why did Wheal Dora have to close down?' she asked.

He shrugged. 'The usual reason,' he said. 'It was cheaper to bring in the tin from Malaya and later on from Australia. It wasn't economic to use our own mines any longer, so—

all but one or two—they were closed down and left to rot.'
She heard bitterness in his voice.

Until now the mine had meant nothing to Kate. She had merely been curious to see the site of this new project of Damian St Ewan's, the venture that was going to bring him in more millions to add to the ones he already had. But now she was beginning to believe that there was far more involved than money and she felt faintly ashamed.

'Why is it called "Wheal"?' she asked. 'Does it mean something special?' She saw the way his brows rose, as if he were wondering if she was really interested or just being polite. 'Tell me about the mine,' she said. 'I'd like to know about it—*really*.' It seemed suddenly vitally important that he should believe that.

Then she saw him smile faintly and she relaxed.' "Wheal" is Cornish for mine,' he said. 'In the great days of Cornish mining there were Wheals all over the place—hundreds of them. Wheal Vor, Wheal Jewell, Wheal Damsel——'

'They sound too pretty to be mines.'

'They weren't pretty.' His tone was grim. 'They must have been very near hell for the men who worked in them in those days. It was a harsh, brutal life. God knows how they stuck it, but Cornishmen have always been tough.'

And you're a Cornishman, and goodness knows you're tough, she thought. I believed you were just a smooth tycoon, a man who sat behind a desk with a battery of telephones. How wrong could you be? 'But it isn't like that now?' she said. 'Modern methods and machinery must make it easier?'

'Mining is always mining. However much technology comes along to help, you'll never be able to put kid gloves on to work on the rock face. The underground miner considers himself the élite of his profession and, by God, he's right. But we've learned a lot recently. New mines have been opened and old ones, like Wheal Dora, are being prospected again. If we can raise minerals from under our own soil in this country and give work to our own men, then it's a job worth doing.' He spoke seriously, passionately almost.

Kate stayed silent, hoping he would say more. With a kind of shock she knew that she wanted to know how he felt about it all. She wanted to know everything about him, every little thing. It seemed extraordinary and wrong that she didn't.

When he spoke again it was as if he was talking to himself, re-living it all. 'I came here almost before I could walk,' he said. 'My father used to bring me. He would sit on this stone here and take me on his knee and talk to me about the old mine and how he knew there was plenty of tin left down there and how he was determined that some day the old place would start up again. I grew up with the one purpose overriding everything else. The time I finished at university was the time that interest in Cornish mining was beginning to revive. My father was alight with enthusiasm— we both were. We had geologists and engineers here and reports were promising. I went to the Camborne mining school to specialise—which is where my brother Mike is studying now. We began to make practical plans for financing the thing. Everything seemed to be sailing along the crest of a wave. And then'—his voice was suddenly harsh— 'then my father had to die.'

Kate swallowed and said nothing—what was there to say? It was very still in this quiet, empty place with the crumbling old buildings looming up beside them. Then somewhere in the darkening sky a night bird shrieked, the cry turning to a wail as it flew on into the distance.

Damian said, 'You may as well know the rest of it now. I should have told you before. Three years ago our house, the old Trestenak, burned down. I was abroad when it happened. When I got back I found there was nothing left but one or two bits and pieces that are in the small library now. My mother and father were in the house with a couple of servants. My mother thought Jet was still inside and she ran back to find him. My father went in after her. They were both overcome by fumes and they died later that night in hospital. As it happens Jet was sleeping in the stables.'

She stared at him, too shaken to speak. She knew all about the deadly cold loneliness of a loss like that. She touched his hand and felt the tension in him. 'I'm sorry,' she whispered. Sorry for what? For him, in that remembered pain? For making him bring her here when he hadn't really wanted to? Sorry that she had seen behind the barrier of suave confidence and cynicism that he must have built up round a wound too deep to be borne? Sorry for her own stupid prejudice that had made her misjudge him so crassly? A little of all of those things. Sorry—sorry—sorry —she felt tears on her cheeks.

She was afraid he might push her away and retreat even further behind his barrier. But after a moment his arm came round her and drew her close against him, and she pressed even closer, her head against his jacket, as if she could somehow, without words, convey to him all that she was feeling.

For a long time he held her like that in the empty silence of the moorland. Then he moved and turned her towards him and wound both arms round her. 'Oh, Kate, Kate.' The words were almost a groan. 'You've got me in a weak moment, haven't you?' Then his mouth came down on hers with a reckless passion born of that other emotion. His lips were hard, forcing hers apart, kissing her deeply, demandingly. His hands pulled aside her dress at her neck and moved over her soft skin with a harsh caress. She drew a sobbing breath and knew that her need of him was as overwhelming as his need of her. Her hands were clasped round his waist, under the smooth stuff of his jacket, as she pressed her body against his.

For long moments they stayed like that, straining to-gether almost desperately, and Kate knew this was a Damian she had only guessed at—a dark, wild, dangerous Cornish-man on whom the veneer of civilisation was only skin deep. Then his hands came up and locked on to her shoulders, putting her away from him. 'This won't do,' he muttered thickly. 'This won't do at all, Kate. Come on, we must go back.'

Her knees shook so much that when he released her she nearly fell. She was thankful that it was too dark for him to see her face. 'Come *on*,' he said again, and he turned away from her and started back towards the car. Somehow she managed to stumble after him.

When they were both in the front seat with the doors closed he pushed back his hair and said, 'I'm sorry, Kate, I promised not to take advantage and I broke my promise. Will you forget it?'

Forget it? She nodded, her head turned away from him. She mustn't delude herself that what had happened meant anything more to him than the need of the moment. He had been shattered temporarily by strong emotion and he had turned to her because she was there and she had been willing. Her need was to comfort, his to be comforted, but as their two bodies met and clung an older, more primitive need had taken over. That was all, and it was no good trying to make more of it. She could only hope, as she felt the blood surging into her cheeks, that he had been too overwrought to notice the shameless eagerness of her response.

They drove the few miles back to Trestenak in complete silence.

Marian was waiting for them when they went into the house. 'Hugo and I have had our meal,' she said. 'We didn't know how long you'd be at the Olivers'. Did you enjoy it?' She grinned at Kate. 'I bet you knocked 'em all with that super dress!'

Damian answered for her. 'Kate was the star of the party. She made all the other women look wishy-washy. Only she'd be too modest to say so herself, wouldn't you, my lovely?' His arm was round her shoulder, squeezing her tightly. So easily could he revert to his usual role, that of the mocking, casual lover, by whom nothing was taken too seriously. Until this evening she had wondered if that side of him was all; if there was nothing deeper. But not any longer. She had seen into the depths of the man, and loved him for what she saw. And now she wanted to be alone, to remember for a little while the moment when he had turned to her, to make believe that she meant something more to him than just a girl he had hired to do a job of work.

She looked down and saw a twig of dried, bleached heather caught in the hem of her white dress. She surely hadn't collected that in the Olivers' drawing room and she hoped that Marian hadn't noticed it.

But Damian had. He bent down and picked it off, twirling it between his finger and thumb, saying wickedly to Marian, 'That's a bit of a giveaway, I'm afraid. You see, Kate and I sneaked out of the party early.'

Marian smiled knowingly, and Kate thought, Don't tell her you took me to Wheal Dora—please don't. Let that be something special, just between the two of us. It was special to Kate and if he didn't mention it she would know it was special to him too. But he said, 'I took Kate out to look at the old mine.'

She felt as if he had thrown a bucket of cold water over her. She heard Marian saying what a good idea, and wouldn't it be marvellous if it could all be started up again. She heard herself agreeing, saying all the right things, and she didn't look at Damian. 'Would you think me very rude if I skipped dinner?' she said to Marian, and added with a little grimace, 'I've got a bit of a headache and I feel like going straight off to bed. Too many of the Olivers' lethal concoctions, I expect.'

Marian looked concerned. 'Of course, my dear, you go up right away. I'll bring you something light—some sandwiches and a glass of nice cold milk, how would that do? And there are aspirins in the cupboard in your shower-room.'

Damian kept his arm round her. 'You should have told me before, we could have come straight home. Poor sweet, I should never have thrown you in at the deep end like that. I forgot how overpowering the Olivers' set can be.'

'It doesn't matter,' said Kate tiredly, remembering how he had raged at her before because she hadn't looked as if she were enjoying the party. How easily he could lie if it suited him!

'I'll go and make your sandwiches,' said Marian, making a tactful exit, and Kate drew herself out of Damian's grasp and turned to the stairs.

'Goodnight,' she said.

He was frowning and he looked puzzled—something very rare for Damian. 'Have you really got a headache?'

Kate said, 'Why should I say I have if I haven't?' And let him take that any way he liked.

'You should have told me before,' he said, and he sounded genuinely worried. 'We could have come back home, instead of——' His eyes were very dark, reminding her. 'All right,' he said, 'you go off to bed and eat your sandwiches and I'll look in later to see how you are and say goodnight.'

'You don't need to,' said Kate hastily. 'Anyway, I'll probably be asleep.'

'Then I shall be able to see how pretty you look when you're asleep. Fiancé's privilege,' he added with his devilish grin. And although Kate turned her back on him and marched up the stairs and into her room, she could feel his eyes following her until her door was closed.

Marian arrived with a tray almost as soon as Kate was in bed. 'There, eat that up and you'll feel better. Did you take the aspirins?' She stood beside the bed like a kindly nurse.

'Yes,' said Kate. She laid her head against the pillow and realised that she really did have a headache now. That's what you got for telling lies. 'Stay and talk to me for a bit,' she pleaded. 'Tell me about the Graysons. I haven't seen them yet.' And if Damian comes and finds Marian here perhaps he'll just go away again.

Marian perched on the end of the bed. 'They're rather dears. From the North—blunt and no-nonsense. She seems capable—she worked in a big house in Cheshire before she

127

married. That must be a few years ago, but she still likes to talk about it. Mr G. has been a gardener all his life, parks mostly, but he can drive and his wife says he's "proper good with his hands," ' she mimicked, laughing.

Kate said, to make conversation and keep Marian there, 'It's lucky they've come just now. There'll be a lot of extra work when the Canadian people arrive on Friday.'

Marian pulled a face. 'Too true there will. Everything's got to go just right with this visit, Damian's banking on it.'

For some obscure reason Kate felt the need to argue about that. 'I can't see why it should make all that much difference. I mean, surely if the Canadian company think the deal is worth going ahead with, then that's all that really matters.'

Marian burst out laughing, good-naturedly. 'It's well to be seen that you're not a business man's wife yet, Kate. Myself, I went through the training very early in our married life, when Hugo had his own company. My dear, take the word of an old hand, when you have a deal to put through, every smallest impression counts. I suppose you could argue that it's immoral, but people are only human, and sometimes a good meal, a pleasant background, can tip the balance between a "yes" and a "no".' She chuckled. 'Look at all the lovelies that are provided to add interest to the motor show, or the boat show. It wouldn't be the same without them.'

Kate smiled faintly. 'I'll have to start learning, won't I?' Marian wasn't telling her anything new; in fact she could probably have told Marian a thing or two about big business. Sometimes the men who worked in it were ruthless and hard and egocentric, sometimes they weren't. You shouldn't judge. She was surprised how much her attitudes had changed in the last two or three days.

She drank up her milk and finished the last sandwich and Marian took the tray, standing up. 'Don't worry, it'll all come quite naturally in time. And Damian's crazy about you, anyone can see that. You won't do anything wrong in his eyes. Sleep well, my dear, and I hope you're feeling better in the morning.' She smiled goodnight and went out.

Kate lay back, her heart beginning to beat uncomfortably fast. Had Damian been serious when he said he intended to come and say goodnight to her? She wished now that she had put on her other nightdress, the one with the short frilly sleeves. It was prettier than the pale blue satin one she was wearing; also it covered up more of her. This one had a classic line, with deep revers to an outrageously plunging neckline. It had once formed part of her trousseau. She thought now that if she had really loved Roger and been heartbroken when he left her she couldn't have kept the nightdress and worn it. She pulled the revers together and looked round for a pin or a brooch—something to secure them. She had a little pearl brooch in her leather make-up case on the dressing table that would do.

Agitatedly, she pushed back the bed covers and swung her feet round. At that moment there was a knock on the door and she swung them back quickly, pulling up the frothy white duvet almost to her chin before she called weakly, 'Come in.'

Damian walked into the room and came and stood at the foot of the bed. 'Feeling any better?' She couldn't be sure whether the words had a sceptical ring to them or not. But then you never could be quite sure, with Damian.

'A little, thank you,' she said politely. She stole a glance at him. In the light from the bedside lamp he looked even taller and broader than usual. On his velvet jacket, near the shoulder, there was a pale smudge. Could that be where her cheek had rested, out there on the moor? She shivered convulsively.

'Are you warm enough in here?' He moved nearer, looking rather helplessly round the room as if he could conjure up some extra heat from somewhere.

'Y-yes, thank you. Quite warm enough.' She pressed her teeth together to stop them from chattering. It was terrible, the effect this man's presence had on her nerves.

He stood looking down at her, close to the bed, and she thought he was smiling, but his face was in shadow and she couldn't be sure. 'Why all the bundling up, then? Maidenly modesty?' He put out a hand and tweaked aside the duvet. Kate only just managed to stop herself from grabbing the satin revers in a ridiculous panicky gesture. Frantically she strove for some sort of poise, but his nearness was causing the most devastating tumult inside her. The thudding of her heart was like a muffled drum-beat in the quiet room. She was sure he must hear it.

'Yes,' he said softly, 'you're beautiful. He'll be a lucky man.'

'W-who will?' she stammered, her dark eyes wide.

'The one you choose in the end,' he said. 'The farmer— or the doctor—or the vet—I'm sure you'll think up some more worthy and altruistic callings to add to your list.' He sounded amused.

He moved away and went and perched on the edge of the dressing table, swinging one long leg. 'What I really came to see you about, Kate—apart from inquiring after the state of your health, that is—was to tell you that I'll be away tomorrow. A crisis has blown up in one of my companies and I have to fly up north to sort it out. I may be back tomorrow evening or I may not—it all depends on the man who usually pilots me. But I'll be back for sure Friday morning, before the Lindsays are due. I promise I won't let you down, I'll be here by the time they arrive. Everything's organised, I've arranged to have them met at Heathrow and then they're coming on here by helicopter.' He smiled. 'Train travelling isn't much in Warren Lindsay's line.'

Kate sat up in bed and hugged her knees. That way she could disguise the inadequacies of the blue satin nightdress. 'You won't want me to do anything, then?'

The smile broadened. 'Only look as pretty as you do now, that shouldn't be difficult.' This was the suave, urbane Damian back in control again. That other man she had glimpsed out on the moor might never have existed.

She said, 'Do they know—about me, I mean? Are they expecting to meet your fiancée?'

'Oh yes. I conjured you up in Canada, just as soon as I saw that it was going to be necessary to take evasive action. Of course,' he added blandly, 'you only existed as a idea at that time. It wasn't until I was flying back home that the idea took on human form and became Miss Kate Warrington.'

'And this girl—Madeleine Lindsay—she still wants to come here even though she knows she's not in the running for the big prize? You?'

She thought his face hardened a little. 'Don't pretend to be cynical, Kate, it doesn't suit you.'

She bit back a smart reply; there was no point in starting another quarrel. She remembered how suddenly that other quarrel had blown up out of the blue. 'Well, does she?' she asked again.

He didn't answer for a moment. Then he shrugged. 'Apparently. Do we have to discuss this in detail?'

'Oh, I think we do,' Kate said. His discomfiture was giving her confidence. 'After all, it's the only reason I'm here at all, isn't it?'

He slid off the dressing table and came across the room to stand beside the bed again. Go away, pleaded Kate silently, please go *away*. But every part of her body seemed to melt into desire for him to lean down, to take her in his arms. For the first time in her life she was powerless, defenceless, against the strong current that ran through her. Her senses were running wild, out of control. The longing was all of her.

She looked up at him almost fearfully, her eyes meeting those liquid dark eyes of his, half hidden by their incredible curving lashes, and she saw by the little smile on his mouth that if she was out of control, he certainly wasn't.

'The way you look at present,' he said softly, 'could suggest other reasons why you're here, but that's a forbidden topic, isn't it?'

He waited for a little while and then, when she didn't speak or move, he said, in his mocking voice, 'Goodnight, then. Goodnight, sweet Kate.'

He could have touched her. It wouldn't have been out of place for him to touch her hand or her shoulder, or even to kiss her lightly as he had done at first, but he didn't. He simply nodded, smiled that maddeningly urbane smile of his, and went out of the room.

Kate lay back on the bed limply, tension relaxed. She had kept her pride; she hadn't let him guess how she felt about him. It would be terrible if he imagined she was making some sort of claim, as the result of his momentary weakness out there by Wheal Dora. Madeleine Lindsay might be hopefully chasing him back to England, although she knew he was engaged. Carole Oliver might be insolently refusing to believe in that engagement at all, assuring herself—and him—that he would return to her in the end. There was probably quite a line-up of other girls waiting to stake a claim.

But not me, Kate said aloud, twisting the great single diamond on her finger round and round. She knew how it felt to be rejected by a man and she wasn't going to invite that again, not in a million years.

She would do her best to act the loving fiancée to Damian, if that was what he needed, while the Lindsays were here. She would get Nanny installed in her cottage and see her happily freed from worry about the future. And then she would go back to London, and the flat, and her good job with Mrs Ashbrook. She would get over Damian, because you had to get over the disappointments and the pain; she had done it before and she could do it again. She would even fashion herself a new dream somehow, but it would be lonely for a while. Cornwall had been her castle in the air for so long. She had found it, and lost it again because she had given her heart to the unattainable master of the castle.

She began to giggle at her own highflown fancies, pleased that she had the resilience to make laughter out of what was material for tears.

The tears came later on that night, and lasted much longer.

CHAPTER EIGHT

THE next day stretched ahead flat and endless, without the possibility of seeing Damian walk into a room or of hearing his car pull up outside. Kate had spent a ragged and unrefreshing night and she was grateful to Marian for sending Ida up with her usual toast-and-coffee breakfast on a tray. While she was dressing she decided to spend the day cleaning the cottage. There was nothing like hard physical work for taking your mind off things you didn't want to think about, and it would fill an empty day nicely.

By the time she arrived downstairs Mrs Grayson, the new broom, had gone into action in a big way. In the living room Ida was perched on a stepladder cleaning the windows, while another girl was on her knees polishing the table-legs. Mrs Grayson herself, duster over her arm, came down the stairs from the raised area to be presented to Kate. 'We're doing a proper turn-out of the house, miss, as the master's away and company's expected tomorrow,' she announced with satisfaction.

Mrs Grayson was a small, brisk woman with a high colour and bird-bright eyes, which she now turned with interest upon Kate, the girl who—she believed—would shortly become mistress of the house. If only she knew! Kate thought. She felt as if she had suddenly been thrown back to the days before her father died, when she really was mistress of a big house, being waited on by servants, consulted by the housekeeper and the cook. She had told herself that she was finished for good with that sort of life—that it was shallow and insincere and that she wanted none of it. How defensive and childish could you be, if you'd been hurt? It was a relief to admit that more than anything in the world she wished she could really be the future mistress of Trestenak, preparing to entertain Damian's important business acquaintances, sharing his hopes and ambitions, loving and being loved by him. That thought, and the impossibility of its ever becoming reality, gave her such a strange sinking feeling inside that she had to pull herself together quickly and think of one or two pleasant remarks to address to Mrs Grayson, whose expression of reserve quickly changed to one of approval.

'I think we may have a treasure there,' Marian said as she and Kate went out to the kitchen. 'She's got Ida moving at the rate of knots already, which I couldn't manage to do. And she knows quite a bit about catering too, although she hasn't actually been a cook. Yes, I believe we've struck lucky and I'll be able to leave you with a clear conscience when the time comes.'

'You're really planning to go, then?'

Marian nodded happily. 'Just as soon as you and Damian are married we'll be off on our own. Hugo and I talked over finances last night and he's even heard of a house outside Truro that sounds just what we want. So things are working out splendidly.'

'Yes, aren't they?' said Kate, rinsing out her breakfast cup at the sink. Then, to her relief, the conversation was ended by the arrival of a delivery of meat for the freezer. She waited for a while in the hope of being helpful to Marian, but soon it became apparent that she was being more of a hindrance than a help—although Marian would never have said so—and she finally armed herself with some cleaning implements, put some lunch together for herself, and escaped to the cottage, borrowing Marian's little car for transport, and Jet for company. The heatwave was still continuing, and the little cottage was full of sunshine as Kate brushed the floors and scrubbed out the kitchen cupboards and cleaned the electric cooker until it was gleaming white. But the cottage had been left in good order by the last tenant and there was a limit to the amount she could find to occupy herself with. She tried to concentrate, while she worked, on how Nanny would love the cottage and how lucky they had been to get it, but that train of thought inevitably led to Damian. The sight of Jet, snoozing in the open doorway, had the same effect with an even more poignant flavour to it. Worst of all, when she

134

took her lunch sandwiches out through the gap in the hedge at the bottom of the small garden and walked a little way into the moor, she found she could see the top of the Wheal Dora stack, standing pencil-like against the blue sky. She turned her back on it to eat her lunch, but it was no good. It was still there behind her and the moment of yesterday was still there too. Damian St Ewan was in her mind and her heart and her blood and she didn't see how she was going to get him out again.

She spent the remainder of the afternoon trying to do just that, to no avail. Mrs Norris, back from shopping, saw the car and came in to see if she could help. Today she had an interested look in her eye that Kate was beginning to recognise. Had the news of the 'engagement' reached the village already? Mrs Norris was a kind soul, but Kate jibbed at the prospect of receiving more good wishes and congratulations that she wasn't entitled to, and after a few exchanged pleasantries she called to Jet and drove back to Trestenak, where cleaning operations were still in progress.

'The study's all finished and ready for you, miss,' called Mrs Grayson from half way up the staircase, and Kate went in there and phoned Nanny.

Nanny was still riding high on a cloud. 'I have to keep pinching myself to believe it's true, Miss Kate. Mr Fogarty and his wife are being so kind. They're doing everything for me, you'd never believe it.' I would, though, Kate thought. Any agent of Damian St Ewan would be the ultimate in efficiency; he wouldn't tolerate any other kind. 'I'm busy packing up already,' Nanny went on, still sounding bemused. 'I think the van will be coming for my things on the twenty-fourth, that's just over a fortnight off, and Mr Fogarty is going to drive Monty and me down himself so as we'll arrive before the van gets there. I can't wait to see the cottage, Miss Kate, and I'm so grateful to everyone. Isn't it lucky for me that you went to Cornwall to work for Mr St Ewan? Mr Fogarty seems to think a lot of him; he must be a wonderful man.'

135

'Oh, he is indeed,' agreed Kate, and it gave her an odd pleasure to say that and mean it.

The rest of the day passed somehow. Kate joined Marian and Mrs Grayson for an impromptu cup of tea on the end of the kitchen table and watched Mrs Grayson's well-trained reserve melting into affability as she saw that Kate wasn't the stuck-up kind. Mr Grayson, a tall, stooping, silent man, was called in from the garden and drank his tea standing up, as far away from Kate as possible after his wife had very correctly introduced them. But even he became less taciturn when Kate discovered that he had a passion for rhododendrons and was able to dig out of her memory the names of one or two choice varieties they had had in the garden at home.

'George'll be in his element with you, miss,' Mrs Grayson beamed, when he had returned to his work. 'The last family we were with didn't know a rhododendron from a rhinoceros, he used to say.'

Kate and Marian laughed at this and Marian poured out second cups of tea and it was all very friendly. By the time Kate went to bed that night she had decided that Damian wouldn't be able to fault her approach to his staff, however much he might complain about the way she had behaved to his friends. Perhaps she *had* seemed awkward and ungracious at the Olivers. Carole Oliver had the ability to get under her skin and make her bristle like a kitten. But she was resolved it wouldn't happen again. Tomorrow, when the Lindsays arrived, her real test would begin, and from now on she would act the adoring fiancée to the limit of her ability, being charming to his guests, helping him all she could towards the successful outcome of the Wheal Dora project. Madeleine Lindsay might prove a bit of a problem if she were still thinking of trying to get Damian for herself, but that hurdle would have to be taken when they came to it. At any rate she wouldn't come unprepared; he had already explained that he was engaged.

As she climbed into the beautifully soft white bed Kate giggled to herself. What a lot of trouble the man took to

136

keep away from matrimony! And what a trail of bruised feminine egos he must leave behind him wherever he went! Perhaps, after all, it was merely her own ego that was involved; perhaps if she could manage to stand outside and watch herself playing a part to the best of her ability, a part that would end when the run of the play finished, it would make the whole thing more bearable. Perhaps, when she saw him again after thirty-six hours, she would find she wasn't in love with him at all.

Perhaps——

Next morning, after breakfast, Kate did the flowers. Flower arranging was one of the skills she had learned during her year at finishing school in France—a year which her father had insisted on, in spite of her protests that she had already spent quite enough time at school, and that she really didn't want to be 'finished'. But in the end she was glad she gave in, for she enjoyed it all hugely and found it not at all old-fashioned and snobbish, and, most important of all, she learned how to run her father's house for him, smoothly and competently. It was sad, she often thought, that he hadn't lived long enough to enjoy her expertise. Now, after three years of living in flat-land, she once again had the opportunity of using the social graces she had learned.

By eleven o'clock she had nearly finished the final bowl, a simple arrangement of long-stemmed cream rosebuds in a tall crystal vase, and was admiring her handiwork, at the same time as she kept one eye on the window overlooking the courtyard where Damian's car would drive up. She had taken a good deal of trouble over her appearance this morning. She had washed her hair last night and now it shone like black satin, curving round her ears. She had chosen to wear a dress of crisp glazed cotton in an olive-green and white print with a perky stiffened jabot tied in a bow at her neck. Already her skin had taken on a faint tan and the whole effect, she had assured herself earlier this morning, was worthy of Damian St Ewan's future wife.

At three minutes past eleven she heard his car coming up

the drive and her heart began to thud uncomfortably. But she mustn't weaken now, she must keep up the act she had chosen. Remembering her classes in deportment she walked smoothly to the door and across the forecourt, reaching the Daimler as he was getting out.

'Darling, you're back—how splendid!' She reached up cool arms round his neck and kissed him.

As she stepped back he looked around, eyebrows raised in mock astonishment. 'Well, well, what a change is here! I don't see any appreciative audience. I thought we became a loving couple only in public—those were your terms, I seem to remember. Don't tell me you've actually fallen for my charms in earnest?'

She tilted her head and grinned up at him impishly. 'That would be something you hadn't bargained for, wouldn't it? No, if you want to know, I'm just practising. I've decided that it will be easier to keep up the act if I think myself into the part. So I've been trying to convince myself that you really are the man of my dreams.' He stood looking down at her, a smile in his eyes, the sun on his hair, and she thought with an almost physical pain in the region of her heart, Thirty-six hours has made it worse, not better.

'Don't you think it's a good idea?' she inquired rather lamely, when he went on looking bemused.

'What? Oh, yes. Yes indeed, a very good idea. I just needed a moment to adjust to the change.' He reached inside the car for his overnight bag. 'So you missed me, sweetheart?' The words were honeyed.

'Desperately!' She closed her eyes, heaving a deep sigh. 'Jet and I have been inconsolable.'

Jet had been standing beside them whimpering hopefully while this conversation was going on, and thumping his tail against the car door. Now Damian reached down to pat his head and stroke his neck while he writhed in ecstasy. 'Have you looked after my lovely Kate, you old ruffian?' He straightened up. 'She is indeed looking lovely this morning,' he added, his smile embracing her, from her sleek dark hair to her tan sandals.

They turned to the house and Kate linked her hand through his arm. 'Seriously, did you manage to straighten things out to your satisfaction in—wherever you've been to?' she inquired.

'Leeds,' he said. 'Yes, I think we've got the problem licked. Just as well I went up there myself, though. I've got certain doubts about the management of that particular company. I'll have to keep a closer eye on things.'

We're talking like a married couple, Kate thought as they walked up the steps to the house together. It meant nothing to him, of course, except that someone was taking an interest in his business activities, but to her it was dangerously sweet to pretend to be part of his life. The way he responded to her gesture in linking her arm with his, pulling her closer against him, was dangerously sweet too. In fact, the whole situation was becoming full of the promise of black misery for her in the very near future. To her horror her eyes suddenly flooded with quick tears of self-pity.

He looked down and saw them. 'Why, Kate, what's the matter? Don't tell me you're that much overcome with joy at my return?'

She sniffed and grasped at a semblance of sanity. 'That would be too realistic altogether. No, nothing more romantic than a midge in my eye. I felt it go in.'

'Let me see.' He took out a clean handkerchief and examined her eye gently. 'This one, is it? No, I can't see anything there now. Does it feel better?'

She blinked once or twice. 'Yes, I think it must have gone, whatever it was.' The nearness of his face to hers was having an upsetting effect on her breathing.

'Good.' His face came nearer; then he kissed her gently, deliberately. He took his mouth away a mere inch or two. 'Hullo, Kate,' he said with unmistakable intimacy.

She searched his face, panic-stricken. This didn't sound like play-acting, but if it weren't then what was it? From this distance she could see the tiny lines round his eyes, the way his dark hair sprang crisp and wiry at his temples, the quizzical line of his mouth, the hint of a cleft in his chin. She had a treacherous longing to reach up and pull his head down so that his lips met hers again, not gently but with the kind of passion they had shared out there on the moor.

She must be mad, she thought, and she made her voice light, coquettish. 'Hullo, Damian,' she returned.

He held her for a moment longer, his eyes passing over her face in a questioning way. Then, with a little shrug, he dropped his arms.

It was at that moment that Marian appeared at the front door, her face ashen. Damian took one look at her, then stepped forward, immediately alert. 'What's happened, Marian? What's the matter?'

She put a hand to her throat. Her blue eyes were wide and frightened. 'The quarry ... an accident ... Fred just phoned. They think it might be ... Hugo ...' her voice died away in a strangled sound.

Damian gripped her arm. 'Get into the car,' he said tersely, and she stumbled into the passenger seat. He closed the door and went round to the other side. Then he seemed to remember Kate. He paused a moment, one hand on the handle of the driving door, frowning down at her.

'You'll have to——' he began. Then he shook his head impatiently and slid in behind the wheel. The powerful engine sprang to life and the car began to back round.

'Damian——' Kate cried as he checked to change gear. He glanced briefly out of the car window at her. 'W-what about the Lindsays?' she stammered.

'To hell with the Lindsays,' he said between set teeth, and the big car swept away down the drive and out of sight.

The helicopter arrived just before midday. Kate had been prowling about the terrace, ears alert, ever since Damian and Marian drove away. She wanted quite desperately to know what had happened at the quarry, but there was no way of finding out without the risk of making a nuisance of herself, so she did the next best thing: she waited for the guests to arrive. If Damian couldn't be here then she would do her best to keep the St Ewan flag flying on her own.

The helicopter slowed, hovered, then descended noisily to pancake on the lawn. Kate went towards it, her hair blowing in the air turbulence, and stood at a respectful distance.

The pilot, a fair young man in denims, jumped out and ran towards her, ducking under the giant slowly-revolving blades. 'Morning, miss.' He had a nice grin. 'A couple of passengers for you. Right?'

Kate nodded. 'I'm expecting them.'

'I'll have to unload and leave them to you,' he said. 'I'm late on my schedule. Afraid they're not either of 'em in very good shape. I tried to get them to rest and come on later, but the old fellow's not the type you can argue with.' Grimacing, he turned back to the helicopter, where a bulky man in shirt sleeves was struggling to help down a girl in a pale green dress who seemed to be swaying from side to side and clutching the door frame.

'Let me, sir.' The pilot lifted the girl down and half carried her across the lawn to Kate, who helped him to lower her on to the grass. Kate knelt beside her, supporting her head, while her father approached, walking slowly and with evident care.

The pilot deposited several items of lightweight luggage beside them and stood for a moment, looking worried. 'Can you manage?' he asked Kate.

'Of course.'

He looked relieved. 'Okay, then, I'll be off. Goodbye, sir, I hope you'll feel better.' He saluted and sprinted back to his machine. Moments later the helicopter had lifted off and was buzzing away into the distance.

Kate, still on her knees, looked up questioningly at Warren Lindsay. 'Travel-sick,' he grunted briefly. 'Always takes her real bad.'

Warren Lindsay was a striking-looking man with thick, cropped white hair and bushy dark eyebrows, and at this moment he wasn't looking any too good himself.

The girl in Kate's arms moved and moaned faintly. She was lightweight and ethereal as a wood nymph with her pale fronds of hair and spiky dark lashes lying against cheeks that were at the moment almost as green as her dress. She opened huge eyes and closed them again. 'I think I'm dying,' she moaned plaintively.

Kate looked round for help and saw Grayson on the terrace. She lifted her voice. 'Grayson, bring one of those small white chairs over here, will you? Now, Mr Lindsay, you sit and rest for a few minutes while we help your daughter into the house.'

He lowered himself into the chair, peering up at Kate under his bushy eyebrows. 'Thanks.' She saw he was economising with his breath.

By this time Mrs Grayson was on the scene too. Between them they got the girl into the house and on to one of the lounge seats built in to a cool corner of the living room.

'You leave her to me, miss, and go and see to her father,' Mrs Grayson told Kate. 'One of my own girls always got like this if she as much as stepped into a car. Very sorry for herself she was, too.' The keen small eyes held a sympathetic twinkle.

'Shall I get her some brandy?' Kate asked. 'I know where the drinks are kept.'

'Better not. She's probably taken those travel-sickness tablets.' She looked up at her husband. 'Grayson, you go and get me a glass of water from the kitchen and then fetch me a blanket from the big cupboard outside our bedroom.'

Reassured that Mrs Grayson could safely be left in charge of the prostrate Miss Lindsay, Kate went across the room and poured out a small brandy for her father. It was a forlorn little picture that she saw as she reached the door on to the terrace: the wide space of open lawn with the sun pouring down, and right in the middle of it a large man in shirt sleeves sitting in a white garden chair that looked much too small for him, surrounded by various items of luggage.

'How are you feeling now, Mr Lindsay? I've brought you some brandy in case you'd like it?'

He sipped the drink gratefully. 'Good girl!' he murmured faintly. He didn't open his eyes. 'Stay here a bit, will you?'

It was intensely hot in the middle of the lawn, far from the shade of the trees. If Warren Lindsay sat here long he would be adding sunstroke to his other miseries. Kate looked round desperately and saw the big garden umbrella on the terrace. Running to it, she fumbled with the unfamiliar levers and catches and finally managed to pull it out of its stand and carry it back to where Mr Lindsay was sitting. Without its heavy, anchoring base there was no way of keeping it vertical except holding on to it herself, which she did. She held it for what seemed like hours, until her arm ached and she felt like a Guardsman outside Buckingham Palace.

At last Warren Lindsay moved, gave a deep sigh, and opened his eyes. 'The old man is himself again. Thank you, my dear, that brandy just about saved my life. I finished the last drop in my flask on that helicopter.' He looked around him dazedly. 'Madeleine?'

'Mrs Grayson, the housekeeper, is looking after her in the house, Mr Lindsay. I'm sure she'll be all right soon.'

He nodded feebly. 'You're all very kind. No way to arrive on a visit—giving you all this trouble.'

He looked so despondent that Kate felt sorry for him. She patted his arm gently, hanging on to the giant umbrella with her other hand. 'Don't worry, Mr Lindsay, it isn't any trouble. We just hope you'll both of you feel better soon.' Her voice was warm with sympathy. 'Damian was terribly sorry he couldn't be here when you arrived. There's been an accident at his quarry and he had to drive over there earlier on. I'm sure he'll be back to welcome you as soon as he possibly can. He asked me to apologise for him.' She remembered his final remark as his car swept away and could have laughed.

'That's okay,' said Warren Lindsay. 'Too bad about the accident.' He peered up at her under his bushy brows. 'And you're his girl, are you? He told us all about you, I'd have known you anywhere. Dark, he said. Dark and lovely, with diamonds in your eyes. I liked that; it sounded good and poetic. I'm hooked on poetry myself,' he confessed. 'Surprised?'

Kate shook her head slowly. After all that had happened lately she felt that nothing would surprise her any more. But who had Damian been describing?

Mr Lindsay's brows were wrinkled. 'Forgive me, I've forgotten your name. Must be the heat.'

'Kate,' she told him. 'Kate Warrington.'

'Ah yes, Kate, of course. I remember now.' He nodded in a pleased way, just as if he really did remember, and wasn't merely being polite and friendly. 'Well now, Kate, I'll move my old bones back into the shade. Can't keep you here holding that great heavy contraption.'

'Are you sure you feel well enough?'

He assured her that he did, that his near-collapse had been merely exhaustion after prolonged travelling, and that so far as his doctors told him he was as fit as the next man of sixty-one. 'And if you're thinking,' he went on, 'that I'm too ancient to have a daughter Madeleine's age, I'm inclined to agree with you, but these things happen sometimes. I'm a foolish old man with one solitary chick and she's everything to me. All I've got.' He smiled fondly.

Kate laid down the umbrella and helped him to walk slowly across the lawn. She was beginning to understand some of the pressures that had caused Damian to arm himself with a mock-fiancée before he met the Lindsays again. It wouldn't be easy to explain to a man like this that you didn't want to marry his beloved daughter.

When they reached the terrace Mr Lindsay chose a chair in the shade. 'I'll stay here for a while, I always feel better in the open. Don't worry about me, I'm fine now, my dear. Maybe you'd go and see how my Madeleine is and come back and tell me, will you do that?'

Kate arranged a cushion for him and turned towards the long window into the living room, but just at that moment she heard a car coming up the drive at the front of the house. Not the Daimler, though, this was no smooth purr but the tigerish ger-rrumph of a super-charged sports car. Oh, *please* not Carole Oliver, Kate prayed, hurrying along the terrace and round the side of the house. Anyone but Carole Oliver at this moment!

But the low, racy car that was pulling up in the forecourt was not Carole's red one, but a citrus yellow, and the driver who was easing long legs out of it was tall, slim, dark, and definitely masculine.

They stood and looked at each other. There was no mistaking the resemblance; Damian must have looked just like this ten years ago—young, fit, exuberant, with everything going for him. That was before events happened that put the lines around his eyes and the irony in his voice. 'You must be Mike,' Kate said, holding out her hand.

He took it in a warm grasp. 'And you must be Kate. My brother gave me the news when he phoned yesterday.'

'Were you surprised?'

'Surprised! It threw me completely off course. Old Damian getting himself engaged!' He gave a small embarrassed laugh. 'Sorry, that sounds rude—what I mean is, nobody expected him to get married, not for years yet. But now I've seen you, Kate, I understand all,' he added gallantly.

She smiled, liking this curiously unsophisticated young man immediately. 'Damian didn't say you were coming home so soon. I'm afraid you've arrived in the middle of an emergency.' She sketched the position in a few words and he looked grave.

'Oh lord, poor old Hugo, I hope he's okay. He doesn't have the best of luck and he's such a good chap. We all think a lot of him.' He looked questioningly at Kate. 'What would you like me to do? Shall I drive over to the quarry straight away and see what the score is?'

'Oh, I wish you would, Mike,' she said gratefully. 'It's awful, not knowing anything. But perhaps you'd better meet the Lindsays first. Damian was so keen that their visit

145

should go off without a hitch, and now everything seems to be going wrong.'

He glanced at her admiringly. 'You seem to be coping pretty well, I'd say. Okay, lead me to the Lindsays and I'll try and stand in for my illustrious brother,' he added with a good-natured little grimace.

Kate led him round the side of the house and along the terrace to the place where Warren Lindsay was resting in the shade, and introduced the two men. Mike St Ewan held out a hand with his frank smile. 'Kate tells me you've had a rotten journey, sir. It's too bad my brother isn't here to greet you himself. I've only just arrived down here from the north and heard the bad news about the accident at the quarry.'

'Bad indeed!' Warren Lindsay nodded his cropped white head slowly. 'You don't know the score, then—how bad is it?'

'No, not yet. I thought I'd drive over there and find out how things are. Better than phoning. Then I'll be straight back to report, unless I can be of any use there. Sorry to dash away, sir, but I'll leave you in my future sister-in-law's hands.'

A twinkle appeared in the keen, perceptive eyes of the Chairman of the Vestor Corporation of Canada. 'And very pretty and capable hands they are too. She has given us a kind and thoughtful welcome and we're obliged to her, my daughter and I.'

Mike transferred his smile to Kate. 'I'll have a word with Miss Lindsay, then I'll be off.'

She led the way through the long window into the living room and across to where Madeleine was lying on the velvet lounge, her legs half covered by a fluffy white blanket. Mrs Grayson had disappeared.

Madeleine's head rested on a dark blue satin cushion, her fronds of pale hair disposed against it in graceful disarray. Her face was exquisite, her skin perfection, her mouth a dream. Looking down at her, Kate saw that even the long spiky dark eyelashes were her own. They lifted slowly now

146

to disclose enormous sea-green eyes, which fell immediately upon Mike.

'Damian!' she whispered huskily. And then, with a tiny frown, 'No—no, you aren't Damian.'

'Certainly not,' said Mike, staring bemused at this vision on the sofa.

Madeleine pulled herself up with surprising alacrity, considering that only minutes before she had decided that she was dying. The fluffy blanket fell aside and she swung a pair of gorgeous long legs over the edge of the cushioned seat, gazing up at Mike limpidly. 'Who are you, then?'

'Michael St Ewan, at your service. Unless,' he added with a grin, 'I'm the prince who wakens the Sleeping Beauty. Know the old fairy tale?'

She pouted charmingly. 'Of course I do. We're quite civilized in Toronto, you know—we can read.' She dimpled. 'I've always understood the prince wakened the Sleeping Beauty with a kiss, though. What went wrong?'

Mike was quite equal to the occasion. 'I must have missed my cue. Shall we go back and play that scene again?'

Madeleine pursed her lovely mouth. 'Some other time, I guess,' she murmured with a glance towards Kate.

'That's a promise.' Mike was looking at the Canadian girl as a collector might look at some rare and precious object he had just found—as if he couldn't believe his luck. 'I've got to go now, but I'll be back. Don't go away, will you?'

She smiled at him under her long lashes. 'What do *you* think?' she murmured.

He stood for a moment as if he couldn't tear himself away. Then he turned abruptly and rushed out of the room.

Madeleine Lindsay sighed and stretched bare, golden-brown arms above her head. 'That Mike is quite something,' she purred. 'And when it comes to looks he's got his brother beat, right from the start.' Then she seemed to remember who she was talking to. 'But you wouldn't agree, of course. You're Damian's girl, aren't you? He told us all about you when he was staying with us in Toronto, and I sort of heard what you said just now when we were tipped out of that god-awful helicopter. Gosh, did I feel sick? How's my loving parent, by the way?'

'Better, I think. He's out on the terrace, resting.' Kate found herself liking this girl. She had the same directness as Carole Oliver, but in Madeleine it was appealing, whereas in Carole it was aggressive and rude.

'I'll go and prop up the old darling, then,' his daughter said. 'That woman who was here said she'd make us some coffee to pull us together.' She got to her feet. Now that she was not sagging she was quite a tall girl—tall and slender and lovely as she stood there smiling, in her mint-green linen dress. What did Damian want, for heaven's sake, if he could turn down the chance of a girl like this, with all the advantages that a marriage into her family would undoubtedly bring him? Ah well, Kate would never know the answer; he wasn't a man who revealed his inner thoughts easily. How he must have regretted giving himself away to her out by the old mine! 'This won't do,' he'd said. 'This won't do at all——' and he had almost pushed her back into the car. She thought now that he hadn't only been meaning the impulse he had had to make love to her, but his own emotional give-away that had led to the impulse. Inevitably she re-lived his kisses, as she had done a hundred times since, and her cheeks went warm.

Mrs Grayson came in with coffee. 'Black, like you said, miss,' she said to Madeleine. 'I hope it's as you like it. I was with an American family for a time, and they showed me how they liked coffee. They said the English couldn't make it right.'

'Thank you, I'm sure it'll be grand.' Madeleine smiled at the housekeeper and Kate thought, she's nice as well as beautiful. How wonderful if she and Mike——

'I've brought a cup for you as well, Miss Warrington,' came Mrs Grayson's matter-of-fact voice. 'I thought you might be needing some. Grayson's taken the luggage upstairs. And lunch will be ready for you when you're wanting it, if you'll let me know.'

Lunch! Kate had forgotten all about food; so much seemed to have been going on. But now she remembered her role as a hostess. 'Thank you, Mrs Grayson. I'll take the coffee—we'll have it outside with Mr Lindsay.'

'Very good, miss.' The housekeeper handed the tray to Kate and went back to the kitchen.

Mrs Grayson had been as good as her word—the coffee was certainly good and strong. Rather too strong for Kate, though both the Lindsays seemed to appreciate it hugely. 'Best cup of coffee I've had in your country,' Warren Lindsay told her. He leaned over and patted her hand kindly. 'Now, don't you bother about us, my dear. I can see you're worried about your young man and this accident and everything. Just let us fit in until things straighten themselves out, and not be a nuisance, eh, Maddie?'

His daughter nodded. 'Yes, of course, Pops, just as you say.' Her huge green eyes were fixed dreamily on a point far away above the tall rhododendrons that fringed the lawn. Kate didn't have to use much imagination to guess where her thoughts were.

When they had finished their coffee Kate took the Lindsays up to their rooms and left them there, resting. Then, somewhat anxiously, she returned to the kitchen to see how matters stood there, since Marian's abrupt departure. She found Mrs Grayson, her small spare form clad in a flowered pinafore, directing the lanky Ida as to the best way to scrape new potatoes.

'Lobster soup, baked ham with salad and new potatoes, followed by raspberry cream gateau, miss, that's what Mrs Harris was going to serve for lunch. I expect you'll want me to take on the cooking?' Mrs Grayson announced briskly.

'Oh, would you, Mrs Grayson, for the time being?'

'That I would, though it may not be as fancy as you'd like. I can cook most things, but I've not been trained to arrange menus in a house like this.' She glanced round the superbly-fitted kitchen, her bright, birdlike eyes obviously approving of what she saw. 'It's all very nice, I'll say that.'

Kate smiled. 'I'm sure you'll do very well, Mrs Grayson.

Your coffee has already won the approval of our guests—they think you're a marvel.'

'Do they indeed?' Mrs Grayson looked pleased. 'Well, if you'll help with the planning and ordering, miss, I daresay we'll keep things going.'

'Of course I will, and we'll hold the fort together until Mrs Harris gets back. We'll have lunch about one, if you can manage that. There will be three of us and Mr Michael St Ewan when he gets back from the quarry—he's gone off to find out what's going on there. I'm not sure when Mr St Ewan will come home.'

'Very good, miss.' Mrs Grayson's manner held just the right amount of respect due from a well-trained upper servant to her mistress. Kate remembered the type from the old days and, although since then she had become accustomed to the more modern free-and-easy relationships between those who served and those who received service, she sensed that this woman would not expect or appreciate a relaxing of the social code.

'Thank you, Mrs Grayson, it's good of you to take it so well,' Kate told her.

Mrs Grayson's red cheeks reddened even more, with pleasure, and she folded her hands across her pinafore. 'I hope I can give satisfaction, miss.' And then suddenly she forgot to be primly correct. 'Oh, Miss Warrington, I do hope Mrs Harris's husband will be all right,' she blurted out. 'The poor soul looked proper knocked over when she left.'

'I hope so too.' Kate warmed towards the little woman. 'I'll let you know when I hear anything.'

Feeling vastly relieved, she left the kitchen. That was one hurdle safely crossed. Mrs Grayson was a good sort; she was willing and capable and it would be safe to leave the cooking in her hands and devote herself to the important matter of playing hostess to the guests. For some reason Damian's words came back to her: 'All you will have to do is simply *be* there when the Lindsays arrive and smile at me now and again.' It wasn't working out quite like that. A wry little smile touched her mouth. 'Just at present you're getting more than you're paying for, Mr Damian St Ewan,' she murmured. Then her mouth went soft and her dark eyes were very bright, because against all the odds, and although he didn't guess it and never would, she loved him until her love was like a pain deep inside her. And money didn't enter into it anywhere.

Mike returned as they were finishing lunch. He dropped into his seat at the table beside Kate, avoiding the three pairs of eyes fixed on him and looking faintly self-conscious, as if he had been rehearsing what he intended to say.

Mr Lindsay was spokesman for the waiting group. 'Well, my boy, how are things? Is it serious?'

Mike looked up then. He was pale but his voice was steady as he said, 'It might have been worse. My brother has things in hand now and there's no further danger, he's pretty sure of that.'

'What happened—trouble with the blasting?'

'No, praise be, not that. There was quite a nasty fall of slate, apparently. I don't know exactly what happened. They've just taken on some new lads and a couple of them were larking about when the foreman's back was turned. Somehow they got one of the trucks adrift and it came down off the rails, dislodging a loose heap on the way. One of the boys was trapped underneath. Another fall seemed imminent and the manager there went in himself to get the boy out.'

'Hugo?' whispered Kate.

Mike compressed his lips. 'Yes, Hugo. He managed to get the lad out to safety, but he wasn't so lucky himself.'

Kate caught her breath. She was only dimly conscious of the two visitors, sitting silently on the opposite side of the table. 'He's not—Hugo's not—dead?'

'No. He's in hospital in Truro. One of his legs has taken a pretty bad mauling. They don't know yet whether there's any other internal damage—they've got to X-ray. They're probably going to operate on the leg as soon as they can, to try to save it. Marian's staying at the hospital and

Damian's backwards and forwards between there and the quarry.' Mike looked over to Warren Lindsay. 'He asked me to tell you how sorry he was not to be here and said he'd be back just as soon as things are sorted out.'

The big Canadian looked doubtfully at his daughter. 'I'm wondering if we should take ourselves off, Maddie, it seems we're kind of redundant here just as things are.'

'Oh no, sir, please,' Mike broke in earnestly. 'We'd all be shattered if you felt that was necessary.' Although he spoke to Warren Lindsay, to Kate it was as if his words were directed at Madeleine, who had said nothing but whose enormous green eyes had not left Mike's face since he came into the room.

'What do you think, sweetheart?' her father asked.

'Oh, please let's not go, Pops. We needn't be any trouble and it wouldn't be friendly to renege just because there was a crisis on hand. *You* wouldn't want us to go, would you, Kate?' she appealed.

Kate smiled back at the girl. 'I don't know how I'd ever face my fiancé again if I let you go,' she said, and to Warren Lindsay, 'Damian's told me a little about your business here, Mr Lindsay, and I know how much he's been looking forward to seeing you and showing you round and discussing matters with you. It would be a terrible disappointment to him if you let this accident interfere with your plans. Do, please, stay and let us make you as comfortable as we can.'

Warren Lindsay's eyes twinkled under his bushy brows. 'How could we refuse a request so graciously expressed? But you mustn't treat us as special guests, please. Let us just fit in with the family in this difficult time.'

'Oh, goody!' Madeleine squeezed her father's arm and her green eyes were bright as they sought Mike's and saw the look he gave her in return. She jumped to her feet. 'I,' she announced, 'am going to start being "family" right now this minute. Yes, Kate, I insist. I expect you've got lots to do and Pops can have a lovely snooze on the terrace. I shall see that Michael here has a proper lunch, and we can get to know each other properly.'

Her father pulled himself to his feet. 'Why do I put up with a daughter who orders me around?' he complained fondly, turning to the window on to the terrace and taking a cigar case from his pocket. 'May I smoke, Kate, my dear?'

'Of course.' She followed him out, looking back to see Madeleine heaping ham and salad on Mike's plate, her pale hair sweeping his cheek as he grinned up at her.

The Canadian caught the direction of her glance. 'No sooner met but they looked, no sooner looked but they loved,' he quoted with a chuckle. 'Your Mr Shakespeare must have had my daughter in mind when he wrote *As You Like It*.' He sank into his chair and lit his cigar thoughtfully. 'Maddie's got a yen for Englishmen, it seems. She took quite a fancy to *your* young man, you know, when he was with us recently.' He chuckled again, reminiscently. 'She did her best, I must say, but he made it quite clear that his affections were otherwise engaged and that he wasn't to be lured away. Polite but firm, that's your Damian.' He smiled appreciatively. 'I like a man who knows what he wants and means to get it.'

'You describe him very well,' said Kate. Damian, who had planned this whole situation in detail, from the moment he had sensed danger! Damian, who would never be diverted from a purpose, once he had made up his mind! And yet, this morning, he had driven off without a backward glance when Hugo was hurt, apparently tossing aside as of no importance this visit that had meant so much to him. No, she would never understand the man.

Warren Lindsay was peering up at her through the smoke of his cigar as she perched on the balustrade. 'I think,' he said contemplatively, 'that your Damian is a very lucky young man. You love him very much, don't you?'

She opened startled eyes. This wasn't the tough businessman, this was the romantic, the man who was 'hooked' on poetry, the man who was sensitive enough to see through to the truth of things.

'Yes,' said Kate softly. 'Oh yes, Mr Lindsay, I love him very much.'

Damian would be pleased with her for sounding so convincing, for doing so well the job she was being paid for, but he wouldn't be pleased at all if he knew she was telling the simple truth: he would be bored and embarrassed. Once the Lindsays had returned to Canada her job would be over and she would go back to London and he would let her go.

She touched her fingers to the lips he had kissed, so often lightly in make-believe and mockery, but once with passion and need.

Yes, he would surely let her go when the time came. To hope for anything else would be sheer madness. But just now she could help him and she would do that to the best of her ability.

Warren Lindsay was silent for a time, concentrating on getting his cigar going to his satisfaction. Then he looked up at her. 'Tell me,' he said, and his voice was different, more incisive. 'You're the one who knows him best. Just why is this mine deal so important to him?'

'How—how do you mean?' Kate stammered.

He shook his head at her surprise, smiling faintly. 'I'm not asking you to give away business secrets, Kate, even if you know them. I'm asking your own opinion. I'll admit right away I lean towards advising my corporation to go ahead with this venture. Damian St Ewan argued his own case pretty well when he was visiting with us lately, and his facts and figures back him up. Internationally he's talked about as a coming man, and he impressed me as someone who knew what he was up to. But he must have many other interests which would be a less risky bet financially than this one, so I ask myself just why he's so steamed up about it. Do *you* know, Kate?'

She felt quite hollow inside. She couldn't interfere—she dared not, and it was horribly unfair of this man to ask her.

'Couldn't you ask *him*?' she stalled.

'Oh, I have. And got the predictable reply in terms of dollars and pounds sterling, as one financier to another. But I get the idea there's something else motivating the man and I want to know what it is. I have to know what makes

154

a man tick before I go into business with him.'

When she still didn't reply he said quite gently, 'I'm not being devious about this, Kate, I don't do business that way. I promise you won't be prejudicing anything by giving me your own opinion. *Is* Damian St Ewan a man who is solely dedicated to business—to succeeding? There's nothing to be ashamed of in that, I assure you. Most of my best friends are exclusively money-motivated.'

Only a couple of days ago she would have had to agree that Damian was of that breed. But now she knew better and she couldn't bear it that Warren Lindsay shouldn't know the truth. She said slowly, 'Wheal Dora has always belonged to Damian's family, Mr Lindsay, I know that. I know that it was closed down for economic reasons, like many other tin mines in Cornwall, and I know that Damian's father dedicated himself to re-opening it, to bringing back some of the prosperity and pride in accomplishment that Cornwall seemed to have lost. He brought Damian up to believe in the idea, right from the time he was a little boy. He went into it wholeheartedly, worked for it, studied for it. Then, when things seemed to be taking a turn here, when new mines were slowly coming along and old ones being examined to see if they were worth re-opening, Damian's father died and he was left alone to—to keep the dream alive.'

Warren Lindsay was looking at her with narrowed eyes. 'Go on,' he said.

Yes, she had to go on now she had started, and suddenly she felt reckless, as if in some way she were pleading a cause, as if the outcome affected herself vitally. 'Damian would probably rather die than admit it, Mr Lindsay, but at bottom he's an idealist. He could so easily have let it go, if he hadn't cared, and concentrated on other interests, as you said. But I'm sure it's much more than a financial matter. I'm sure he saw the old mine brought to life again as a modern unit, men working here under new, better conditions that bore no resemblance to the bad old days of dirt and danger. I'm sure he could almost hear the turbines throbbing away, the ore coming to the surface, the village being re-born, cottages being built or restored. It wasn't just making money, or being successful, it was something deeper, something——' She broke off, flushing. 'Sorry, I let myself get carried away. I didn't mean to sound sentimental. Damian would never forgive me.'

She gazed anxiously at the big, powerful, important man sitting opposite. His expression told her absolutely nothing. This, she thought, with a sinking feeling inside, was the look he would have when he had regretfully to put a veto on someone's hopes and suggestions.

'Thank you, Kate,' he said, and when he stood up she felt as if she had been interviewed and was now being dismissed, 'you've told me exactly what I wanted to know.'

Oh lordy, she thought, what have I said? Butting into Damian's business affairs like a Miss Fix-it! She could almost hear her father's voice saying, 'Your job is to look delightful at the head of my table, Kate love. Leave me to do the talking.' She should never, never have let herself be carried away by Warren Lindsay's probing, however delicate it had been. Gloom and guilt settled round her like fog.

'Mr Lindsay,' she began, 'I didn't mean to——'

But she never knew what either of them would have said next, for that moment the telephone rang in the study and she flew to answer it.

CHAPTER NINE

She lifted the receiver, her heart thudding anxiously. 'Trestenak,' she announced, and Damian's voice said, 'Kate?' He sounded strained.

'Yes.'

There was a slight pause. 'Has Mike got back yet?'

'Yes, he's having lunch.'

'Then you know about Hugo? Mike told you he may have to lose a leg?'

She swallowed hard. 'Yes.'

'They're waiting for X-rays and tests before they operate. I'm staying around with Marian for the moment.'

'Yes, of course,' she said. And then, 'How is Marian?'

'Being wonderful, as you'd expect,' he said briefly. 'Her sister's on her way from London to be with her. I shan't be able to get away for some time yet though, even when I leave here—things to clear up over at the quarry. Everything all right with you?' He sounded detached.

'Yes,' she said. 'The Lindsays arrived.'

'Mike told me. He'll have to do his best to cope until I get back. No need for you to get involved in all this, Kate.'

Get involved! I'm in it, she thought, up to the neck. But this was no time to tell him. He wasn't really here in this gracious world of Trestenak just now. He was in a different world, an enclosed world, a world of hospital smells, of endless waiting, of fear and pain, of comforting and being comforted.

'I'll do what I can,' she told him.

'Yes, yes, I'm sure you will. Is Mike there—can you bring him to the phone?'

'I'll do that,' she said. She wished he didn't seem to be shutting her out. 'Damian—I——'

She stood for a moment, biting her lip. Then she put the receiver down and went to look for Mike.

For twenty-four hours nobody at Trestenak, including Kate, saw anything of Damian. Then he came home, looking grim and weary. So weary that Kate's heart melted at the sight of him and she longed to have the right to put her arms round him and comfort him. He greeted his guests, apologised for his absence when they arrived, and announced that the operation was over and that so far as the doctors would say at present Hugo's leg would be saved.

Then, apologising again, he went to bed, asking not to be disturbed, and slept until dinner time, after which he and Warren Lindsay were closeted together in the office until long after everyone else in the house had retired.

That was how it was for nearly a week, with Damian coming and going and wearing such a preoccupied look that Kate didn't dare to approach him, and they were never alone together because he spent every unoccupied moment he had, deep into the night as well, with Warren Lindsay.

'Too bad you're not seeing much of your young man, Kate,' Mr Lindsay commiserated with her. 'He and I have a lot to go into, and he's got other things on his plate as well.'

'I know,' Kate said. 'I don't mind.'

The big man nodded as if that was what he would have expected her to say. 'When you marry a man you marry his job, if it's a man like Damian St Ewan,' he mused. 'Is that an old-fashioned point of view?'

'Perhaps,' she smiled. 'But I think it's still fifty per cent true, at least.' It could be a hundred per cent for a girl like me, she added silently, amazed how much her point of view had changed in such a short time.

'It depends on the man, eh?' Warren Lindsay's keen eyes twinkled at her.

'As you say, Mr Lindsay, it depends on the man,' replied Kate.

She hadn't realised how much she was enjoying being mistress of Trestenak, doing all the things that Damian's wife would do. Planning meals, ordering and supervising deliveries, attending to the comfort of the guests, sorting the laundry, arranging the flowers, showing interest in what Grayson was doing with the garden, which, he grumbled, had been 'let go' lately. Mrs Grayson was willing, and had turned out to be a good cook. Kate brushed up her year's training in France and produced some exciting sauces and trimmings. All in all, she congratulated herself, her side of things was going smoothly. She didn't expect praise from Damian; she didn't even expect him to notice what she was doing. But she was hungry for a word with him, with just the two of them alone, and when he didn't make the opportunity she dared to do it herself.

He had returned from his office at midday and he and Mr Lindsay had had a working lunch in the study. Mike had taken Madeleine out sailing—they spent most of their time together at present—and Kate had had a solitary lunch. From the window she saw Damian going out to his car and ran after him.

'Damian, just a minute!'

He rolled down the window and waited courteously, but with a touch of impatience, she thought.

Now she had him alone she didn't know what to say. 'I just wanted to—to ask if everything is all right?'

He smiled, faintly puzzled. 'Quite all right. Why?'

She improvised a little wildly. 'Well, when Marian left I just—sort of took charge, but I wondered if—if——'

He raised dark eyebrows. 'You need a little positive reinforcement, as the psychologists would call it? A few pats on the back?'

'No!' She flushed. 'That wasn't what I meant at all.'

'You mean I didn't engage you as housekeeper and your extra duties are too much for you?'

'Of course not,' she said crossly. This wasn't turning out right at all. 'I merely want confirmation that—that the meals are okay, that your guests are comfortable, that——'

'Everything's fine,' he interrupted, and then, 'Look, Kate, I've got a board meeting at two o'clock.' His hand went to the self-starter.

It served her right, she thought dismally, she should never have intruded into his important masculine world of affairs with such trivial domestic details. She gave him a quick, contrite grin. 'Sorry,' she said, and would have stepped away from the car, but his hand shot out and caught her arm.

'Kate darling, I'm taking you for granted, I know. I'm a selfish oaf and you're being wonderful. Go on backing me up, I'm relying on you.'

The pressure on her arm increased for a moment, then he smiled at her, let in the clutch and drove away.

When she turned back to the house it was just as if bells

were ringing, and her arm, where his hand had pressed it, seemed to be on fire.

After that, although nothing much changed in the pattern of the days, time flew by. The weather held in its hot, sunny groove. In the garden there was the whirr of the lawn mower and the ceaseless syncopated cooing of wood pigeons, the scent of cut grass and roses, the cool blues of hydrangeas and delphiniums with here and there a clump of white daisy-like flowers that grew larger and taller than any daisies Kate had ever seen before. Mike and Madeleine went about together, with eyes for no one but each other. And the two small vertical lines between Damian's eyebrows relaxed.

During the second week of the Lindsays' visit he spent more time at home—but always 'in conference'. The big table in the study was littered with maps and books and reports, and papers covered with figures and jottings. The mining industry had evidently not heard yet of women's equality, Kate decided, for the stream of callers that came and went constantly were exclusively male; some in sober business suits, some with tanned faces, wearing denims and bush jackets. Kate never managed to sort them all out, not even their names. She laid on a succession of lunches, sandwiches and pots of black coffee and carried them to the office at Damian's request, to be greeted with amiable but absent-minded thanks. Some of the men stayed for dinner, and one or two overnight, and the talk was always of shipping and smelting, concentrates and price controls, markets and currency. Kate didn't mind that it went on over her head; she was busy and she was happy and she had no time to think. The only time she wasn't conscious of a bubbling-up of happiness was when Mr Oliver, Carole's father, called to see Damian. For some reason he constituted a threat, which was odd, because he beamed pleasantly at her and said that his wife and daughter sent their love. 'Oh, yeah?' breathed Kate somewhat inelegantly to herself as she went to brew yet another pot of coffee. Any

160

mention of Carole Oliver had a disastrous effect upon her spirits.

News of Hugo's progress came by way of Damian, who called at the hospital when he was in Truro, and from Marian, who telephoned several times and spoke to Kate. She was troubled that she had 'let Kate down' and anxious to know how the visit of the V.I.P.s was going along. Kate was able to reassure her. 'As you guessed, Mrs. Grayson's turning out a treasure. Don't you worry about us. Is there any talk of Hugo being able to come home yet?'

There was talk, Marian said, but nothing definite. The operation had been successful so far as they could tell and there had been no internal complications, which was a blessing. It would be some time before Hugo could be mobile, even with crutches, but she kept on hoping they would let him out of hospital soon. 'I'm longing to have him to myself to look after,' Marian added. Now that the crisis was over her sister had returned to London, and Marian was living in a hotel room near the hospital and itching to return to her normal activity.

Kate telephoned Nanny once or twice and was reassured that everything was proceeding in an orderly fashion and she was living for the moment when the van would drive away from the front door and she would follow it into the country.

In short, Kate reflected, as she sat alone on the terrace one evening after dinner, everything seemed to be progressing according to plan. Except for one thing, and that the most vital, to her at least. When this episode was over, what happened to Kate? Only a short time ago she would have answered that question quite definitely. She was going back to London, as far as possible from Damian St Ewan, who had the power to rock her world to its foundations. But now—she wasn't sure. Against all reason, hope was stirring and growing inside her and she wasn't doing a thing to stop it. It dated from that moment he had called her 'Kate darling' and said he relied on her. She sat back in her chair and gazed down the twilit garden, where the mists were rising, and let herself dream a little.

Then a deep voice behind her said, 'Kate!' and her heart leaped and began to thud heavily.

Damian dropped into a chair beside her and let out a long sigh. 'When all this is over,' he said, 'I shall sleep for a week.'

She tried to think of some expression of warm interest that wouldn't sound too inquisitive. 'Are things going on satisfactorily for you, then? I haven't dared to ask, but I've been keeping my fingers crossed.'

'So have I, constantly. I think—mind, I said *think*—I think we may be home and dry.'

'Oh, that's marvellous!'

'Don't hang out the flags yet. Lindsay hasn't committed himself to anything—he's pastmaster of the art of playing his cards close to his chest. But he's got all the gen now, every darned detail he wanted. Tomorrow he's going into purdah, or whatever men do, to work it all out by himself. He's going to give me his decision tomorrow evening. If it's "yes" then he's pretty confident of being able to carry the rest of the Vestor boys along with him. They're a colossal corporation—Wheal Dora would only really be chicken-feed to them. But even so they like to be as sure as they can that they won't lose on it.'

'But you think it will be "yes"?'

His face was in the shadows, but she heard the smile in his voice. 'I don't play a bad game of poker myself. I think it will be "yes". One good sign is that Warren Lindsay seems to have taken to Mike and he's invited Mike to go back to Canada with them on a visit. I can't believe he'd have done that if he'd meant to turn us down flat. It'll be nice for Mike—good experience too. He jumped at it.'

'Of course,' said Kate.

Damian turned his head sharply. 'And what, exactly, does "of course" mean, spoken in that mysterious manner?'

'Haven't you noticed *anything* that's been going on out-side the study?'

He ran a hand through his hair. 'You know very well that

I've been immersed in business for days. I'm a horrid tycoon, remember?' But he was making a joke of it. 'Well, what's been happening that I should know about?'

'While you've been wallowing in money matters Mike and Madeleine have been busy falling in love with each other.'

There was quite a pause. Then, *'Really?'* he said. 'You're sure?'

'So would you be, if you'd been looking around you. Are you pleased?'

'Stunned,' he said. 'But Mike's only a kid—only twenty.'

She smiled. 'So what?' Suddenly she had a feminine desire to delve deeper. 'It looks as if you could have saved yourself a lot of trouble,' she said, and then wished she hadn't said it.

'Trouble?'

'Of bringing me down here to protect you from Madeleine.'

'Oh, that! That was quite different.' Different from what? she wanted to ask, but restrained herself. She couldn't see his eyes, but something she thought she had heard in his voice made her quiver inside and hold her breath, waiting.

But he said, 'The Lindsays plan to fly back home on Friday. They're taking the first train to London on Thursday; Warren Lindsay says he can't face the inside of a helicopter again just yet. So tomorrow will be their last full evening. I think we ought to put on some sort of social "do" for them. Could you cope, do you think?'

It had been wishful thinking, the note she had heard in his voice that had sounded like tenderness. She flushed as if she had been snubbed but braced herself quickly. 'What sort of a "do"? A dinner party?'

'Too formal, and there isn't time,' he said. 'Just the ordinary evening thing—drinks and snacks. You know. If I give you a list could you ring round to people and ask them to drop in? You've met most of the men already, that morning at the Fisherman's. You could explain a bit about

Warren Lindsay—why it's such short notice—you know what to say——'

The perfect secretary, that was how he saw her now. 'Yes,' she said, in a secretary-voice. 'I could do that.'

'And could you manage about the food and everything?' he asked vaguely.

'Yes. That too.'

'Thanks, Kate, you're a treasure,' he said.

'Like Mrs Grayson,' she observed drily.

'What?'

'Oh, nothing. Shall we go in and then you can make out the list and I'll start on the telephoning.'

Dream ended, she told herself as they went into the house together.

There was no time for dreaming next day, even if Kate had had any dreams left that were viable. Immediately after breakfast she and Mrs Grayson discussed plans for the party, and decided that the only way to provide a buffet supper at short notice was to put the whole thing in the hands of caterers.

'Will Mr St Ewan mind the extra expense?' Mrs Grayson was a woman of true north-country economy.

Kate assured her that Mr St Ewan would certainly not mind, and added, in case Mrs Grayson should feel that she wasn't pulling her weight, 'He wouldn't expect you to cope at such short notice. I'll see if I can contact Mrs Harris on the phone. She'll know the best caterers to approach.'

Marian was delighted to hear Kate's voice. 'Of course, I know the very people, here in Truro,' Marian said. 'They've helped us out at short notice before. I could do the arranging for you myself, if you like, but it would be much better if you could come over yourself and explain exactly what you want, and the numbers likely, and everything. It would be grand to see you again too. Could Damian drive you, if he's coming to Truro?'

'I don't think I'll bother him,' Kate said guardedly. 'He's terribly busy just now, as you might imagine.' Actually

Damian had left shortly after breakfast, having first en-
sconced Warren Lindsay in the study with a request that
he should have coffee and lunch taken in to him. Damian
had then gone off without saying where he was going or
when he would be back. But by now Kate was used to his
comings and goings. She knew that Hugo's absence from
the quarry had thrown a great deal of extra work on him,
and thought that was probably where he had gone now.

'I tell you what, I'll borrow your Mini, if I may,' she told
Marian. 'I've got one or two things to arrange with Mrs
Grayson and I want to do the flowers before it gets really
hot, then I'll drive over and we'll meet at your hotel, shall
we? Just give me directions.'

Marian was waiting for Kate in the cool, comfortable
hotel lounge. The hotel was, Kate guessed, the most expensive in Truro, and she also guessed that Damian was insisting on paying the bill.

Marian kissed Kate and said, 'How lovely to see you.
I'm feeling very marooned here, but at least I can see Hugo
every day—usually twice a day.'

'How is Hugo?' Kate asked, and Marian brightened up
and said that the doctor's report yesterday was the best
yet, and Hugo might be allowed to come home in a week or
ten days.

'You must look in and see him for a minute or two now
you're here,' Marian said. 'I'm sure Sister wouldn't raise
any objection, so long as there isn't a surgeon's round on.
But first we'll go and fix up the eats for your party.'

They went out of the hotel and walked along Boscawen
Street and Kate said, 'Truro looks an interesting place, I'd
love to poke about here.'

'That's what I do, to amuse myself, between the times I
can visit Hugo,' Marian was enthusiastic. 'I can't tell you
how much I've learned already about my home county. You
must get Damian to show it all to you, Kate, when things
settle down a bit. He's very well up in the history of the
place. The cathedral's superb, of course, with its three
spires. And Truro was one of the original Stannary Towns

165

of Cornwall, where the officials came from London to test the quality of the tin. They used to chip a corner if they approved of it. But Damian will tell you all about it.'

Kate smiled and said she would look forward to that, and thought with a pang that when things 'settled down a bit' she would be back in London, typing away at her desk in the Ashbrook Secretarial Studio.

Making the arrangements for the party didn't take as long as Kate had thought it would. The name of St Ewan magically brought the manager from his office to give the two girls his personal attention, and for a time mouth-watering words such as lobster, crab and asparagus, paté and vol-au-vent and mousse, black cherries and cream gateau and raspberry sorbet filled the air.

'The drinks you can safely leave to me, Miss Warrington,' the manager assured Kate. 'I know Mr St Ewan's preference.'

She was glad enough to agree, and shortly afterwards the manager showed them out with a cordial and deferential assurance that everything would be attended to, including servers.

'It's all so easy when you're rich,' Kate murmured with a faint curl of her lip, and she saw Marian glance a little oddly at her. That really wasn't the kind of remark you made when you were about to marry a millionaire, for love. But it didn't seem to matter much now, because she wasn't.

Hugo was delighted to see them. 'A buckshee visit!' he exclaimed, grinning all over his nice, freckled face with its shock of red hair. 'Sister said that Mr St Ewan's fiancée had called in to see me, as if you were Princess Anne at the very least. It's made her day.'

He was in a small ward, and Kate felt five or six pairs of interested male eyes upon her at Hugo's hearty greeting, and found herself flushing. To cover her confusion she handed over the grapes she had brought, and said the usual optimistic things, and Hugo was very cheerful, and the five minutes they had been allowed slipped past like a flash.

Then Sister came into the room, immaculate with smooth

hair and gleaming silver buckle on lilac print, and a quick, curious glance at Kate. 'Time's up, I'm afraid. The physiotherapist is here.'

Kate patted Hugo's hand and told him to keep up the good work and Marian kissed him and said she'd be back this afternoon, and they beat a hurried retreat from the ward.

Coming down the corridor towards them was a vaguely familiar figure. When it got nearer Kate recognised the young doctor she had met at the Olivers' party. He stopped to greet them, exchanged a few words with Marian about Hugo's improvement and then turned to Kate. 'Nice to see you again, Miss Warrington. In town for the day?'

Kate shook her head. 'Only briefly, I'm going back to Trestenak now.'

The doctor said, 'And I'm just going off duty now. Join me for a drink, both of you, I've got something to celebrate and nobody to celebrate with. Please, I won't take no. Have you a car here? Then we'll go in mine.'

Within minutes they found themselves back at the same hotel they had left earlier. Dr Turner parked his car and then led them into the crowded bar. 'Now then, what are you two girls going to drink?'

It was very hot in the bar. 'A long gin and lime, please, with plenty of ice,' Marian said.

Kate said, 'The same, without the gin, if I may.'

'Oh no!' The young doctor pulled a face. 'You can't celebrate on that,' and Kate laughed and said she was driving back.

He looked at her with comic disappointment. 'And I was hoping to have the pleasure of driving you home. I'll be going right past the St Ewan place.'

'It's very kind of you, but——'

Marian chipped in, 'Kate, would you mind awfully if you left the car with me, so long as Dr Turner can give you a lift? It *would* be rather useful to have it here, then I could come home now and then, to see you all and how things are getting along.'

Kate said, 'Of course—why didn't you say before? I could easily have got a bus back,' and the other two laughed and said, Didn't she know that Trestenak was off the bus route?

Dr Turner settled them at a table in the window and came back through the crowded bar with their drinks. 'Now for my celebration news,' he said. 'It's just been confirmed that I've got the hospital appointment in London that I've been after for some time. Specialising in gynaecology.'

Marian clapped her hands. 'Babies, how lovely!' and Kate joined in the congratulations, thinking that the young doctor would make a kind and sympathetic women's specialist.

They lingered over their drinks. Toasts were drunk and Dr Turner talked at length about his future hopes and prospects. Kate was beginning to get a little edgy about getting back to Trestenak when Marian, glancing towards the door of the bar, said, 'Oh dear, there's my protegée and I've been keeping her waiting for her lunch. I forgot all about her.'

In the doorway, alone, stood a little woman in a prim, flowered dress, wearing gold-rimmed spectacles and a worried expression. 'Her husband's at the Infirmary too,' explained Marian. 'She's a very nervous type, poor dear, and I've been trying to help her to keep her spirits up. She doesn't like going into the dining room on her own, so I promised to join her.' She stood up. 'Thanks for the drink, Dr Turner, and for what you've done for Hugo. I'll be seeing you soon, Kate. You're staying on in Cornwall for a while?'

Kate hesitated. After tomorrow the charade of the 'engagement' would be over and her services would no longer be required, but it would be up to Damian to manipulate the ending as cleverly as he had manipulated the beginning. And then what? She couldn't think ahead. 'I'm not quite sure what my movements will be,' she said. 'Miss Bebb is coming soon, to take over the cottage. I'll get her installed and then—we'll see.'

Marian nodded. 'I'll go and do my good deed for the day,

then.' She left them to join the waiting figure by the door.

'A nice woman,' said Dr Turner, 'devoted to her husband, and he to her. It's been a bad business for them both and she's been splendid.'

'Is Hugo—will he be completely recovered in the end, do you think? Am I allowed to ask? Or would it be breaking medical protocol?'

Dr Turner shook his head. 'I wish I knew the answer myself—I'd tell you if I did. It was a nasty injury and the surgeon did a first-class job on him, but it's difficult to say yet what the final result will be.' He went into details of nerves and ligaments, becoming quite immersed in his subject until finally he must have noticed the slightly glazed look in Kate's eyes. 'Sorry—you should have stopped me,' he laughed ruefully. 'I'm apt to get carried away when I talk shop, and you're a receptive listener.'

'I'm interested,' she said with a smile. 'But you lost me about five minutes ago. And now I really think I must get back.'

'Another drink before we go?' he suggested hopefully. Kate refused and was relieved when he said, 'I suppose I mustn't either, or I'll never arrive at my patient's house all in one piece.' He stood up and pulled back her chair and guided her through the crowded room, a hand at her elbow. Leaning down, he whispered into her ear, 'Heaven knows how many of my patients have me under scrutiny at the moment. I hope they're not mistaking euphoric intoxication for anything worse!'

She looked up into the thin, intelligent face with the humorous blue eyes and laughed. 'I'll be your witness for the defence, if you need one.'

Giggling together companionably, they went out to the car.

Afterwards, Kate recognised that that was the day when everything happened at once. Threads that had been hanging loose suddenly decided to tie themselves into knots, or fly apart, whichever way you looked at it. Mike and Madeleine had been out for lunch and they came back in the late afternoon and disappeared together into the study, where Warren Lindsay was still installed with his books and papers. Later, they all three emerged on to the terrace, where Kate was snatching a quick cup of tea, in between preparations for the party.

She got up. 'Tea, anyone else?'

She doubted if they heard her. The two young people had eyes and ears for nobody but each other, and Warren Lindsay was beaming benevolently upon them.

He turned the beam upon Kate. 'Do you happen to know if your young man is anywhere around?'

'I haven't seen him since early this morning. I think he went to the quarry.'

'We have news for him.' Keen eyes twinkled under bushy brows. 'Perhaps now I should finish that quotation from William Shakespeare that I began the other day. You remember, Kate? "No sooner met but they looked, no sooner looked but they loved, no sooner loved but they sighed, no sooner sighed but they asked one another the reason, no sooner knew the reason but they sought the remedy." ' He chuckled. 'It seems we have another engaged couple in our midst,' he announced happily.

Just then Damian came out on to the terrace. When he heard the news he was all elder brother, clapping Mike on the back cheerily, kissing Madeleine, shaking hands with Warren Lindsay. It seemed to Kate a kind of afterthought when he drew her into the circle—a family circle it was now, but Kate wasn't 'family'. She acted up as well as she could, but she was thinking of another engagement that was as false as this new one was true.

'A double wedding, maybe?' Warren Lindsay was suggesting. 'What about it?'

'What about it, Kate?' Damian drew her closer, smiling down into her eyes, and she, and only she, saw the irony in his glance.

'Maybe,' she replied, and looked away from him.

Ida came out of the house then. 'A telephone call from

170

Bristol for Miss Warrington,' she announced, and Kate escaped gratefully to the study.

Nanny sounded excited but slightly anxious. 'Miss Kate, I do hope this won't put you out, but would it be convenient if I moved tomorrow? I know it's a little earlier than I said, but the removal firm say now that it would suit them better. They have a return load they could fit in and that would reduce the cost a little. What do you think?'

'Splendid!' said Kate. And it *was* splendid. The Lindsays leaving tomorrow morning. Nanny arriving tomorrow afternoon. After that Kate would be free of commitments, free of responsibility to anyone. Free to come and go as she liked. Free—and longing with all her heart to be tied to one man.

'I'll be waiting for you, Nanny,' she said. 'It'll be lovely to see you again.'

Just then the van arrived from Truro with the goodies for this evening's party and after that Kate was busy with preparations. This party would be the last time she would appear in public as Damian St Ewan's fiancée, the last time she would be able to do anything to help him, socially or in any other way. It was a trick of fate that the girl she was supposed to be protecting him from was now engaged to his brother, but all that was water under the bridge. The important thing was that Warren Lindsay's visit should finish on a high note, and Kate was going to do her part in making that happen.

Lunch was an al fresco meal, served by Mrs Grayson on the terrace, and afterwards plans for the rest of the day were discussed. Dinner, as a formal meal, was vetoed by everyone, rather to Kate's relief. Warren Lindsay expressed a wish to visit Land's End before he returned home. 'I've already seen John o' Groats, and I guess it's the poet in me that wants to see the other end of this green and pleasant land of yours.' He directed his twinkle at Kate.

'Oh yes, please take us, Damian,' Madeleine chimed in. 'I've been trying to get Mike to show me Land's End, but he said it would be too crowded.' She giggled. 'He seems to

171

have had an idea in his head about secluded coves being better—and he knows them all, don't you, sweetie?' She held up her mouth for his kiss.

Damian looked at Kate. 'What about you—darling?' There was something in his look, in the tone of his voice, that made her a little uneasy, but she pushed the thought away. He was probably a bit tensed up, waiting for Warren Lindsay's decision.

'I'd love to, but I'm afraid you'd better count me out,' she said. 'I think I should be here to keep an eye on things before our guests arrive.'

He didn't try to persuade her, and a little while later they all drove away, saying that they would probably have a drink, and a bite to eat, on their way back.

That left Kate free to concentrate, and by the time she was ready to go upstairs to shower and change she was satisfied that the spacious room looked fit for any party— even a millionaire's party! Against the soft jewel-colour glow of the carpets and curtains and sofas, the silver and crystal gleamed and glittered, and in the raised area, on the long dining table, Kate's principal flower arrangement, a bowl of apricot roses which seemed to float in a delicate shell-pink haze of astilbe, picked out here and there with the startling blue of anchusa, made even Grayson remark that she had 'done a good job there'.

Kate stood and took a last look round. The servers had arrived, the food was all ready to be transferred from fridge to table. All was ready for the arrival of the guests. As it was to be an informal party she had no exact idea how many people to expect, but last night's telephoned invitations had been received with enthusiasm, and she guessed that one or two previous dates might well be hurriedly cancelled for the intriguing prospect of a party at the St Ewan residence and the promise of meeting a V.I.P. from Canada.

The invitations had been 'from about nine' and it was now, she saw, a quarter to eight. Nice time to get herself ready and then come down to supervise the final setting-out of the food. She found Mrs Grayson in the kitchen, suitably attired in black silk dress with a white lace collar, and entertaining the servers with coffee and sandwiches.

'I'm going up to dress now,' Kate told her. 'I expect Mr St Ewan and the others will be back soon. If I'm wanted for anything will you send Ida up to tell me, please.'

Earlier in the day she had chosen the dress she intended to wear and now it hung by itself at one end of the wardrobe rail. It was a model, and she had flinched a little at the price, but Louise, Marian's friend, had insisted that it was absolutely right for her and it hadn't just been sales talk! It was long and exquisitely cut in a clear cool yellow crêpe, the colour of wood primroses, that moulded her swelling young figure and fluted out in a demure frill round her ankles. The neck-line was fashionably low, but the cleavage not openly seductive. She had wanted a dress that Damian would approve of and she had guessed that he would not like his woman to look too provocative—in public. He would no doubt prefer to keep her charms for his own delight. The picture that this thought conjured up sent a quiver through her now that was almost pain and she had to shower quickly with clear, cool water to calm herself down. She patted herself dry, admiring the even biscuit-coloured tan that the last weeks had brought to her body, smoothed on skin lotion, draped herself in a filmy white wrap and sat down before the dressing table mirror to make up.

It was while she was taking pleasure in brushing her hair to a raven's wing sheen that the knock came on the door. 'Come in, Ida,' she called.

Reflected in the mirror she saw Damian close the door behind him and stand leaning against it. He was wearing rough canvas trousers and a red and navy checked cotton shirt and his hair was undisciplined. There was nothing of the suave, elegant executive she had first seen in London about him now. He looked every inch a black Cornishman at this moment—and dangerous. Automatically she pulled the flimsy nylon wrap round her body.

173

He sauntered across the room and stood with one arm along the top of the mirror, looking down at her so deliberately that she felt a strong quiver pass through her. 'Don't bother to cover up,' he drawled. 'I'm the only one here, and you're still wearing my ring, you know.' His smile wasn't a smile at all. 'I may as well have my money's worth.'

She was on her feet in a flash, her cheeks burning. 'You promised——'

His fingers dug hurtfully into her shoulder as he pushed her back on to the dressing stool again. 'Yes, I *promised*,' he mimicked. 'All right, my sweet, I didn't come here to seduce you, although'—again that deliberate, disturbing scrutiny—'I must say the idea has its attractions. No, I've just been talking to Warren Lindsay. I thought you were entitled to know the result.'

'Oh?' She was struggling to bring her emotions under control.

'Success, success. He's satisfied, and he's going to recommend his corporation to go ahead.'

'That's wonderful,' she said. 'Splendid,' she added, in case she hadn't sounded sufficiently enthusiastic. She wished his announcement didn't feel like an anti-climax.

'Yes, isn't it?'

'Aren't you pleased and relieved?' she asked, for he didn't sound it. In fact, there was something very odd about his manner—had been from the moment he came into the room—earlier than that, when she came to think about it, from the moment he had turned up on the terrace this afternoon.

'I suppose I am,' he said, 'especially after getting off to such a disastrous start.'

'You mean the quarry accident? But it only delayed things a couple of days.'

'Two days is a long time to a man like Warren Lindsay. He's not the sort to hang around wasting his time for any reason at all.'

'You thought he might leave again when you weren't here? That the deal might fall through?'

174

His mouth twisted. 'Let's say I thought it might die from malnutrition.'

'But you went—you stayed away for two days, nearly.'

'My dear girl,' Damian said tartly, 'it was a matter of priorities. The quarry is my responsibility, and Hugo and Marian are my friends.'

'Yes, of course,' she said, feeling rebuked.

'And of course it all came right, didn't it? You held the bridge for me like a good little second-in-command.'

Her eyes widened. 'I just did what I could.'

'Very efficiently, it seems. You've got Warren Lindsay eating out of your hand. He was getting positively lyrical about you just now. It seems I'm the luckiest.'

She was beginning to feel cold inside. She hadn't expected gratitude, heaven knows, but she hadn't expected *this* either—this contemptuous sarcasm. Was he really so petty, so childish, that he couldn't accept the idea that he had to rely on anyone for help in a business matter?

'Nice for you,' she said briefly.

'Is it?'

'Well, isn't it?' She tried to speak patiently. 'You know quite well that really I hadn't anything to do with it. Warren Lindsay is only being polite—and perhaps a little grateful because I looked after him when he arrived feeling rather groggy. It's what he thinks of *you* that matters, surely? And he must believe you're the kind of man he likes to do business with, that's obvious.'

'Great!' He flared at her suddenly, as he had flared that night of the Olivers' party. 'You've done a grand PR job on my behalf. Feeling what you do about me it must have been pretty galling for you to sell the idea of the big-hearted idealist, Damian St Ewan. The tycoon who cares more for his workers and his dreams than his bank account! Yes, you did very well, Miss Warrington, even if you did exceed your brief more than a little.'

'I see,' she said dully. 'I'm sorry.' And then, because it seemed the obvious thing to say, 'I'll leave here as soon as convenient, of course.'

'May I inquire where you're thinking of going?'

'Why, back to London, where else?' Did he think she was likely to stay around, after this? 'But just to put the record straight,' she added, and looking at that hard, indifferent face it took every bit of courage she possessed to say it, 'I wasn't doing a PR job for you, as it happened. I meant everything I said to Mr Lindsay.'

His mouth was a thin, harsh line. 'You don't really expect me to believe that, do you? You must think me very credulous.'

She gasped at the sheer injustice of it. She had wondered how he would manipulate the ending between them, but she hadn't expected anything quite as ruthless as that he would choose such a paltry thing to blame her for and to quarrel about.

Suddenly anger swept through her and she jumped to her feet and turned on him. 'I don't care what you believe, but it's true. I *did* mean it when I told Mr Lindsay I thought you were wonderful. Anyone,' she added as pointedly and nastily as she could, 'can be mistaken.'

His eyes narrowed, glittering dangerously. 'It seems that you have some difficulty in making up your mind about the sort of man you think I am.'

'No difficulty at all.' She wanted with all her heart to hurt him as he had hurt her. 'I think you're exactly what I expected at first. I think you're utterly contemptible and insincere and—and hateful!'

He took a step towards her and she flinched at the rage she saw in his face. 'You're a good one to talk about insincerity, Miss Kate Warrington,' he said between his teeth. 'But don't forget—whatever you may think of me, for tonight you're still my fiancée.' He took her wrist in a grip that hurt and drew her towards him deliberately and his cotton shirt was harsh against the softness of her flesh. His face was only inches from hers, dark and dangerous, and she found herself unable to move, or draw away. 'Yes,' he sneered, 'I promised, didn't I? But the bargain's broken now—you broke it yourself. So I'm free to take what I can get.' And his mouth came down on hers, brutal and demanding.

When he took it away she heard the quick breathing of his sharp, angry desire as he pushed her down on to the bed, pulling aside her thin wrap. Then his arms were round her, his body against hers, and Kate was helpless—helpless and almost lost in the wild rush of longing that broke over her like a great warm wave. Hardly conscious of what she was doing, she twined her arms round his neck, pressing him closer, giving back kiss for kiss as his hands moved over her smooth shoulders, down her back to her waist.

Then there was a loud knocking at the door.

'Get to hell out of it,' muttered Damian, his mouth warm against Kate's throat.

The knocking continued and Ida's voice, shrill and frightened, called, 'Miss Warrington, Miss Warrington, can you come? The electric cooker's on fire!'

Damian let out a couple of savage words and wrenched himself away and stood up. 'All right, I'm coming,' he shouted with controlled fury. For a moment he stood, looking down at Kate. Then, 'You'd better get dressed,' he said, and the contempt in his voice cut through her painfully 'I shan't be coming back.' And he went out of the room and shut the door.

For a few shattered moments she lay where he had left her. Then she crawled over to the dressing table and surveyed her tangled hair, her too-bright eyes, her flaming cheeks. There was more on fire than the electric cooker, she thought, and began to laugh hysterically.

When she had managed to calm down a little she crept to the top of the back stairs and listened. She heard Damian's voice from the kitchen, then Mrs Grayson's subdued, 'Thank you, sir, thank you very much indeed. I'm sorry to have bothered you. I'll know another time.'

The emergency, whatever it had been, had obviously been dealt with. Kate waited another few seconds. Then she went back to her room and began to dress for the party.

CHAPTER TEN

How she got through that evening Kate never knew. She moved through the beautiful room, full of beautiful people, and her mouth ached with the effort to keep on smiling and her throat ached with the effort not to burst into tears, and the rest of her felt numb, as if she had been anaesthetised. Somehow she smiled at the compliments of the men, somehow she dealt with the interested quizzing of the women, playing it by ear, waiting for it all to be over, longing to get away and never see any of them again.

The only good thing was that the newly engaged couple —Mike and Madeleine—took the glare of the spotlight now. Everyone wanted to talk to Madeleine, beautiful in a floaty, leaf-brown wisp of a dress that blended with her fronds of pale hair and made her look more ethereal than ever.

Damian was keeping up the charade to the end. He stayed close to Kate, convincingly the lover. Miserably she thought that he probably didn't trust her not to let him down again.

Only once were they alone together, although in full view of the rest of the people in the room. Damian gazed down with apparent delight at the clinging folds of pale yellow that caressed her body and swept into foaming waves round her ankles. 'Pretty dress, my sweetheart,' he murmured. 'Very seductive!' The way he said it sounded like an insult. He put his hand to her neck. 'I see you're wearing the pearls at last.' He fingered them slowly until Kate could have screamed at the touch of his hands on her skin.

'Your instructions—to wear them,' she said.

'Ah!' he nodded. 'Very obedient!'

'I'll return them safe and sound—with your ring,' she said.

He took her left hand and lifted it to his lips. 'Sure you wouldn't like to keep it—as perks?'

She smiled up at him brilliantly. 'I hate you!' she snapped, and turned away to speak to one of his friends who was approaching. A few minutes later she saw him disappear through the garden window with Carole Oliver hanging on to his arm, her head tilted provocatively. Tonight she was wearing a pleated apricot chiffon affair with pom-poms dangling from the neckline and waist. A model girl might have carried it off and looked amusing in it. It made Carole Oliver look like a cheap lampshade, thought Kate viciously.

The evening crawled on. There was music and one or two couples danced on the terrace and the lawn. Mike and Madeleine revolved dreamily in each other's arms. Damian established himself near the side table that was serving as a bar and showed no inclination to dance, which was a blessed relief. Whatever he cared to think of her, Kate buoyed herself up with the thought that she was keeping her side of the contract to the bitter end. But if they had danced together, if she had felt his arms around her again, she couldn't have trusted herself not to scream or smack his face, or somehow make fools of both of them.

At last the guests began to leave. Kate stood near the door and said all the right things in a clear, high hostess voice. It helped that she had had a few more drinks than she could comfortably handle. She was going to feel like death later, she knew, but she was going to feel like death in any case, so what difference did it make?

When she decided hazily that everyone must have left by now she escaped to the study and stood holding on to the table, breathing quickly. She'd done it, she'd stuck it out and not made an idiot of herself. All she wanted now was to crawl into bed and pull the sheets over her head.

'Kate!' Damian had followed her in.

She spun round, her eyes wide, but he didn't look angry or dangerous any more. He looked almost as weary as she felt.

'I'm taking the Olivers home,' he said. 'John has had a drink too many and doesn't feel like driving. I just wanted to tell you that I've arranged to travel up to London tomorrow morning with the others.'

She nodded. It took quite an effort, but she said fairly clearly, 'I'll start packing tonight, probably. I'll see Nanny settled into the cottage tomorrow when she comes and then I'll get away myself as soon as possible.' Suddenly her hand flew to her mouth. 'I—I suppose it's still all right—about the cottage, I mean?'

'Certainly,' he said curtly. 'You probably don't believe it, but I assure you that normally I don't go back on my word. Your friend may move in as soon as she likes, and when Hugo is back in charge he'll come and fix up with her about a lease, and so on, as I promised.'

'Thank you.'

He leaned against the bookcase. 'Not at all. Thank *you* for all your assistance. I may stay in town for a while, then I'll be going up north again for a few days, so——'

'So I shall have left by the time you get back?' she said woodenly.

'It looks like it. Maybe I'll see you around some time if you come to visit your friend.'

'Maybe,' she said.

Carole stood in the doorway, all apricot glow. 'Oh, here you are, sweetie. Daddy and Mummy are ready. Coming?' She held out a hand invitingly and Damian took it and let himself be urged away without another look at Kate. They didn't close the door and she stood watching them cross the big, empty room together. As they reached the far end she saw Carole stop and say something, then she reached up and wound her arms round Damian's neck. His arms went round her waist and he lowered his head.

Kate didn't wait for the kiss. Somehow she got out of the study and groped her way up the back stairs, clinging on to the rail as if the floor were lurching under her. When she reached her room she locked the door, just as if anyone might try to come in, and lay on the bed, wanting to die.

By the time she was seeing them all off next morning, she had a strong feeling that she *had* died, and was a small grey ghost among these people who seemed in particularly high spirits. Mike and Madeleine walking on clouds with stars in their eyes. Warren Lindsay, bluff and friendly, holding Kate's hand in both his own and saying earnestly, 'I've been insisting that this young man of yours brings you over for a long visit with us soon, my dear girl.'

And Damian—Damian who wasn't noticeably the joky kind—was this morning joking with everyone, even Mrs Grayson. 'I'm leaving you to see that Miss Warrington doesn't get into mischief while I'm away, Mrs Grayson,' he called as that lady hovered respectfully in the background. Then he took Kate in his arms. 'Au revoir, my love,' he murmured, loud enough for them all to hear. 'Be good.'

For the last time she lifted her face for his kiss, but his lips were hard and hers were cold. Perhaps, she thought ghoulishly, this is the kiss of death. She stood on the steps and waved the Daimler out of sight and they waved back, all except Damian, who was driving, and Grayson, who was sitting beside him to bring the car back.

Mission accomplished, said Kate to herself, and went back into the house to finish her packing. She packed exactly the things she had brought with her. All the clothes she had bought with Damian's money she left hanging on the rail or neatly folded in drawers. She removed the diamond from her finger and put it back in its box. This, with the pearls in their case, she took to the room that she knew to be Damian's. She had never been in his room before, and now she crossed it blindly, placed the two cases on the dressing table, and walked out again.

Then she went down to the kitchen to find Mrs Grayson. A lovely party, wasn't it, Mrs Grayson enthused, quite carried away from her customary taciturnity by all the excitement and comings and goings. Kate agreed that it had been a lovely party and said, 'I'm expecting a friend of mine later today, Mrs Grayson. A Miss Bebb, who's coming to live in one of the cottages down the lane. She's being driven here by Mr St Ewan's agent in Bristol and I'm not sure whether they will come to the house here, or go straight to the cottage. If they *do* turn up here will you please tell them that I've gone to the cottage and will wait there until they arrive?'

'Certainly, Miss Warrington, I'll do that. And what about meals today, miss?'

'Count me out, Mrs Grayson.' The very thought of eating made her choke. 'I've already stocked up the fridge at the cottage; I'll picnic there today while I'm helping Miss Bebb to get straight.'

'Very good, miss. Oh, and Miss Warrington——'

'Yes?' Kate turned back.

The housekeeper fumbled in the pocket of her overall and drew out an envelope. 'Mr St Ewan said to give you this when he'd gone, miss,' she smirked, evidently under the reasonable impression that it was a love letter. 'He said to be sure you got it.'

'Thanks, Mrs Grayson.' Kate went into the study, closed the door, and tore the envelope open. Inside there was a cheque for five hundred pounds, made out to Kate Warrington, and signed Damian St Ewan. Nothing else. She stood for a moment or two holding it, looking down at the firm black handwriting. Then she tore cheque and envelope across, threw them into the waste basket, and went out of the house by the front door, closing it behind her. She would have to come back here to sleep tonight, but after tomorrow she would never see the inside of the house again.

'It's just as I dreamed of it, Miss Kate.' Nanny sat in her own chair, in her own front parlour, with her own cat on her knee, smiling softly and contentedly. Outside, darkness was falling across the lane and the moor beyond. After the heat of the day the cool breeze brought scents from the garden drifting through the open window.

Kate, curled on the window-seat, said simply, 'I'm glad, Nanny. You deserve it.'

Nanny's happiness was worth it all, she kept telling herself. Everything in *this* sector had gone according to plan.

Frank Fogarty had duly delivered Nanny by car, accompanied by Monty.

'Mr Fogarty even got Monty a special travelling hamper,' Nanny explained with a kind of awe at having received so much consideration, and Frank Fogarty had grinned cheerfully behind an enormous drooping moustache and said, 'We aim to please.'

The van with the furniture, he told Kate, should arrive about an hour or so after them. He was sorry not to have seen the boss, but would they mind if he pushed off straight away? He had a client to call upon in Taunton on the way home.

The furniture removers arrived, unloaded, and departed. After that Kate had her work cut out to prevent Nanny from exhausting herself in the excitement of deciding the best possible place for everything. Innumerable cups of tea had helped to slow things down. Now it was nine o'clock; Nanny's bed was made; Monty had been out to explore the garden and dutifully decided to come in again for the night; Mrs Norris from the farm had called in a neighbourly fashion and stayed just long enough to earn Nanny's approval; and now, at the end of the long day, Nanny had suddenly come over tired and had had a little weep of happiness while Kate went to make a final cup of tea before she left.

Now, the pot drained, Kate stood up and collected their cups. 'I'm going this moment,' she said firmly, 'and you need a good night's sleep, Nanny. I'll be down to see you in the morning before I leave for my train, just to make sure everything's all right. It's a shame I have to get back to London so soon, but I'll be back again before you know I've gone.' She laughed brightly. 'That's one drawback to living near the sea,' she teased, 'you never have visitors off your doorstep!'

Nanny lifted Monty to the floor and stood up a little stiffly, a small spare woman who had worked hard all her life. 'You'll always be welcome, Miss Kate,' she said, her voice not quite steady. And that, thought Kate, was the understatement of the year, but Nanny had been trained to keep a tight control over her emotions.

In the little kitchen Kate rinsed their cups and emptied the tea-pot. Then she came back and hugged the older woman. 'Goodnight, Nanny dear, sleep well and be happy.' She was held close for a moment and then, with a cheerful wave, she ran down the front path and out into the lane.

Out of the radius of the lights from the cottages it was very dark. Kate slowed her steps. It was a relief to let go of her smile, but her jaws ached from the effort of keeping it on her mouth all that long day. Now she could weep and there would be nobody to see. But the tears didn't come. She felt dried up all through—dried up and old. Older than Nanny. Her feet dragged as she went on up the lane, between the high hedge banks, towards Trestenak.

Then to her left something moved, a large dark shape detached itself from the bank. Kate felt a scream rise in her throat, but no sound came. She froze to the spot.

'Don't be frightened, Kate,' a familiar voice said.

Damian. Damian, who was in London. She covered her mouth with her hand. They said that when stress got too much for you you saw things, heard voices, that weren't there. There was a rushing noise in her head as if she were submerging under the sea.

But he was there, he was real. 'Sorry about the melodramatic appearance,' he said. 'I've been waiting for quite a time.'

'For me?' she croaked.

'Who else? I haven't yet met your friend Miss Bebb.'

She was beginning to surface again. 'Why are you here? Why did you come back?'

'Because there was a question I hadn't asked you, Kate.' He didn't come nearer, or touch her. 'Let's go on, shall we?'

They walked on up the hill, slowly, with almost the width of the narrow lane between them. When she couldn't bear the silence any longer Kate said, 'What was the question?'

'Ah yes, the question. Why do you want to go back to London, Kate?'

184

She stopped walking. 'W-why do I——' The man was incredible! 'I don't have to answer,' she hedged, a little spirit returning.

'Oh, I think you do.' His voice was deep, almost gentle.

She lifted her chin. 'Very well, then. Because the job you engaged me for is over, and you made it quite clear that you were—were dissatisfied with me.'

'Dissatisfied with you?' He gave a sudden bark of laughter. 'What utter rubbish! Of course I wasn't dissatisfied with you.'

'But—but that's what you said.'

He came nearer and stood looming above her in the near-darkness. 'Kate Warrington,' he said, 'don't you recognise sheer bloody-minded jealousy when you encounter it?'

'J-jealousy?' she repeated stupidly, and, looking up at him, she saw that the first stars were beginning to come out.

'Let's start again,' he said patiently. 'Do I understand that your sudden urge to dash off to London *wasn't* because Dr Timothy Turner is going there?'

Life began to bubble through her veins. 'Of course it wasn't.'

'You're not in love with him?'

'No, not in the least. I hardly know the man.'

'Then,' said Damian, 'would you consider the possibility of taking your ring back and going on being engaged to me? For real this time, Kate. Oh, I know you've got this thing about money and so on—you did a good job of tearing up my cheque, I noticed—but we'd try to get over that small hurdle by degrees, because I'—unbelievably, he gulped and caught his breath—'I don't think I can go on long without you. London was an empty desert. I offered a heavy bribe to a helicopter pilot to get me back here and I've been sitting in that hedge for hours with the cottage under surveillance, waiting for you to come out.' He was fooling, but his voice was still unsteady. 'Kate—will you?'

She couldn't say a word. Her head was spinning, the stars were spinning, the whole firmament was spinning. She went into his arms and he held her tenderly as if she was the

185

most precious thing in the world. He kissed her pale face, pushed back the dark curtain of hair and kissed her cheeks, her temples, her mouth.

He held her away a little at last. 'See? I *can* behave like your Mrs Ashbrook said, like a perfect gent, sometimes. But I'm not making any promises.'

She was grateful for the darkness as she pressed close to him. 'I wouldn't want you to,' she told him. 'I never wanted you to. You knew that?'

'I guessed,' he said. 'A man usually does. We did something to each other right from the beginning, didn't we, Kate?'

'Then why didn't you tell me?'

He laid his cheek against her hair. 'When you aim to catch a butterfly you don't go charging in with a whacking great cudgel, my darling, and you were a very elusive butterfly. Every time I came near you with my net—off you fluttered again. I was never sure of you because you didn't really seem to like me much.'

'I tried not to at first, I was prejudiced, I admit it. But there was a good reason—or at least I thought so. I'll tell you about it some time.'

'Some time,' he agreed, 'but not now. There are more important things to attend to now.' He drew her close into his arms again and kissed her with frank but controlled passion, his hands seeking the softness of her body under the thin stuff of her shirt.

But presently he let her go. 'I can wait,' he said, 'for just the length of time it takes to get ourselves married, not a moment longer. I'm going to Scotland tomorrow—shall we go together? There's a small hotel overlooking a loch that I know. We'll be there together tomorrow night, married if they still do it the old way, over the anvil, or if that isn't possible—will you mind?'

She shook her head. 'I won't mind. Shameless, aren't I?'

He cupped her face in the starlight. 'I love you, Kate,' he said very deep. 'I love you in every possible way. Everything I have is yours to do as you please with. Even Wheal Dora.'

She smiled. 'That's one gift I could never accept,' she said softly. 'But I'd like to share her with you if you'll let me.'

Arms entwined, they wandered slowly on up the hill, towards the dark shape that was Trestenak, her future home. Wonder and delight enclosed Kate like a shining cloud, but there was still one thing that, womanlike, she had to know.

'Damian,' she said presently, 'why did you believe I was going off to London with Dr Turner? It was so utterly and absolutely untrue.'

He thought for a while, then he said, 'How well do you know your Shakespeare? Othello?'

Othello—that sinister story of how jealousy can grow like a canker, fed by lies. 'Ah,' she breathed as a glimmer of understanding came. 'Carole Oliver?'

He drew in his breath. 'I should like to wring her pretty neck,' he said. 'I probably will when she comes back from New Zealand. I imagined she was just an amusing kid, but I was wrong. She's deadly. When she told me that you and Tim Turner were seeing each other, meeting in secret, I laughed at her and told her she was a pretty poor liar. But the hints went on every time I happened to meet her, smiling innuendoes, sly little remarks. Drip—drip—drip—like water on a stone. And I met her pretty often—John Oliver and I do a good deal of business together. I caught myself wondering—remembering that night at the Olivers' house when you'd been with him. I told myself that you were loyal and sincere, that you would never let me down like that—because, in the circumstances, it *would* have been letting me down—but I couldn't quite get rid of the poison, just like that poor devil Othello, with Iago beside him, aiming his deadly little arrows where it hurt most.'

'Go on,' she said, beginning to understand.

'Well, I was longing for the end of the Lindsays' visit—to have the time to get you to myself, to find out the truth. And then, that last day, I was in Truro at lunch-time. I went in for a drink and there you were—you and Turner, sitting

187

together over by the window, laughing and talking and having a whale of a time. You didn't see me, did you? I reacted like the betrayed husband in a Victorian melodrama —drew back into the shadows, watching. What depths we can still descend to! You passed quite close to me on the way out and he was leaning down over you and you were laughing up at him and your eyes were shining. I followed you and saw you get into his car and drive off together. My God, Kate, I was pretty near to murder then.'

She sensed the violence in him, like a living thing, and she had a spasm of cold fear, but she made herself say firmly, 'It was nothing, absolutely nothing. Marian and I were at the hospital, seeing Hugo, and we met Dr Turner and he took us both for a drink. Marian had been with us almost until we left, and he gave me a lift back here so that I could leave Marian's car with her in Truro. I went in to arrange with caterers for the party,' she added.

'Yes,' he said, 'you don't need to explain. I know I was a fool, a jealous, bloody fool. I should have asked you then and there, instead of——'

'Instead of which you were livid with me for saying nice things about you to Warren Lindsay.'

It was wonderful that they could laugh about that together now. And that when they had laughed they had to kiss again, to reassure each other, to wipe out suspicions and hurts.

'I'm not surprised you told me you hated me,' Damian said complacently at last. 'I was fairly vile that evening.'

'You were indeed,' she agreed. 'The worst moment was when I saw you kissing Carole just before you drove them home. Was I intended to witness that?'

'Probably,' he admitted frankly. 'But I wasn't kissing her, she was kissing me, kissing me goodbye before she went off to New Zealand on this trip with Daddy, the little viper. It meant exactly nothing, but—yes, I suppose I wanted you to see. I'm not a very nice fellow, my love. Why do you want to marry me, if it's not for my money?'

They had nearly reached home now. With the familiar night sweetness all round she reached up and pulled down his dark head and whispered her answer in his ear.

It seemed to satisfy him.

Attention: Harlequin Collectors!

Collection Editions

of Harlequin Romances
now available

We are proud to present a collection of the best-selling Harlequin Romances of recent years. This is a unique offer of 100 classics, lovingly reissued with beautifully designed new covers. No changes have been made to the original text. And the cost is only 75¢ each.

Not sold in stores, this series is available only from Harlequin Reader Service.

Send for FREE catalog!

Send coupon today for
FREE
Harlequin Presents Catalog

We'll send you by return mail a complete listing
of all the wonderful Harlequin Presents novels
still in stock.

Here's your chance to catch up on all the
delightful reading you may have missed
because the books are no longer available at
your favorite booksellers.

Fill in this handy order form and mail it today.

Harlequin Reader Service   In Canada:
MPO Box 707,   Stratford, Ontario
Niagara Falls, N.Y. 14302   N5A 6W4

Please send me without obligation my FREE Harlequin
Presents Catalog.

NAME _____

(please print)

ADDRESS _____

CITY _____

STATE/PROV _____ZIP/POSTAL CODE _____

ROM 2075